The Devil's Grip

The Devil's Grip

Lina Wolff

Translated from the Swedish
by Saskia Vogel

OTHER PRESS
New York

First published in the Swedish language as Djävulsgreppet in 2022
by Albert Bonniers Förlag, Stockholm, Sweden
Copyright © Lina Wolff 2022
Translation copyright © Saskia Vogel 2024
Published by agreement with Salomonsson Agency

The cost of this translation was supported by a subsidy from
the Swedish Arts Council, gratefully acknowledged.

Production editor: Yvonne E. Cárdenas
Text designer: Patrice Sheridan
This book was set in ArnoPro
by Alpha Design & Composition of Pittsfield, NH

1 3 5 7 9 10 8 6 4 2

Library of Congress Cataloging-in-Publication Data
Names: Wolff, Lina, 1973- author. | Vogel, Saskia, translator.
Title: The devil's grip : a novel / Lina Wolff ; translated from the Swedish
by Saskia Vogel.
Other titles: Djävulsgreppet. English
Description: New York : Other Press, 2024.
Identifiers: LCCN 2023029952 (print) | LCCN 2023029953 (ebook) |
ISBN 9781635424201 (paperback) | ISBN 9781635424218 (ebook)
Subjects: LCGFT: Novels.
Classification: LCC PT9877.33.O54 D5513 2024 (print) |
LCC PT9877.33.O54 (ebook) | DDC 839.73/8—dc23/eng/20230727
LC record available at https://lccn.loc.gov/2023029952
LC ebook record available at https://lccn.loc.gov/2023029953

Welcome to my house. Come freely. Go safely;
and leave something of the happiness you bring!

—BRAM STOKER

WHEN SHE GETS to Florence, all the couples making love are what overwhelm her first. Together they stroll through arched passageways in the inner city and above their heads run dark, ancient beams. The place is hot and grandiose, nothing like she imagined it would be when once, many years ago, her train had stalled at the station. Then huge snowflakes fell upon what appeared to be a lethargic, cold, brittle city. But now there are all these lovers in the heat. She hears them through the open windows, through the walls of his apartment. A woman's scream, then murmuring soon followed by laughter.

"Is that how people have sex here," she asks, "and around the clock, no less?"

"Yes," he replies. "Is there anything wrong with that?"

"No," she says, "not at all."

It occurs to her that she comes from quite an austere part of the world. It also occurs to her that she has much to learn, and that the man at her side might just be the person to guide her into this new realm. From his terrace the ocher tile roofs spread out before them, and Florence from above appears to be the city of the second chakra. The second chakra is the pelvis, and its color is orange. Orange, ocher, a color in and of this place. Everything seems to be adding up, she thinks. At last it all seems to be adding up.

Sweat clings to their skin like a membrane. She likes the smell of his. She likes everything about him, even though he is so very ugly. He has long, dark, tangled hair, which he draws around his face as if to hide it, but there's no hiding a face like that. She tucks his hair behind his ears. He's ashamed, he says. She tells him not to be; his face adds another dimension to his masculinity, and besides, it's a pleasing discordant contrast to the city's feminine charm. He gives her a wary, almost shy smile. People they pass on the street look him over, then her, then him again. This is a first for him, he says.

"People are staring because they don't understand why someone like you would choose to be with someone like me," he says.

But the women who get it *really* get it, and their interest manifests in a particularly Latin way. On one occasion they're sitting on a park bench, and a woman stops for a drink at the nearby water fountain. She stands alongside him and when she bends forward, her bottom hovers a mere half yard from his face. He gives a satisfied smile.

"This is only happening because I'm with you," he whispers. "They never notice me when I'm on my own."

Here she already considers the possibility that he's lying to her, but she pushes such thoughts away. There he is after all, sitting next to her on the bench, arms comfortably stretched along its back and the smell of sweat rising from his armpits.

There's nothing to worry about. He's harmless, repulsive to everyone but her. He's a harmless little fatty. She will look back on this time and state (bitterly) that there is in fact no such thing as a harmless little fatty.

Soon women start checking him out even more often. She sees the pleasure it brings him, and at first she can't help but smile. After all, she's responsible for this transformation, she's the one driving it. Gathering up all his faded, gray T-shirts and throwing them away. Making sure he buys brightly colored linen shirts, deodorant, and new jeans.

"Jeans," she says, "can make or break a body."

She explains, for example, that stone-washed jeans can't be paired with slightly shiny black dress shoes, the kind with a heel that clacks on the cobblestones.

"It makes you look like a salesman who deals in truck steering systems," she says.

"But that's pretty much what I am," he replies.

Out of embarrassment, she laughs.

"Right, that is pretty much what you are. But what's stopping you from saving those nice black shoes for a funeral and otherwise wearing sneakers?"

He listens and learns. Follows her around the shopping center, buying whatever she recommends. She says that a shaved head might suit him, maybe leaving a millimeter or so of dark shag, like Shane in *The Walking Dead*. He googles it and nods.

"But what about this face?" he asks. "It'll scare people off."

"You'll have a different look about you," she says. "Like

you're not trying to hide anything, like you're proud of your more menacing side."

He obeys. In the mornings she goes running with him through the parks before the heat descends on the city. Slowly his belly fat dwindles. She brings him along to the gym, and while she works her abs on the mat, he's in front of the mirror toning his biceps.

"Without all that hair, I look like *un cazzone*, a giant cock, standing here doing dumbbell curls," he says.

She laughs. She loves it when he's like this, foulmouthed and sweaty, she's starved of people who don't take themselves too seriously. The transformation continues. Salad every night, fruit for breakfast. Plus so much sex that the masculinity is seeping from his pores by the time he leaves the house. In the mornings she stands at the window and watches contentedly (but naively) as her miracle walks out into the world.

PRACTICAL MATTERS REQUIRE their attention. Sooner rather than later, so they know where they stand.

"Sure thing," he says. "I'm all ears."

First and foremost: She's here on a one-way ticket. No, no return flight. She wasn't sure how things were going to turn out. What about her job, he says, she must have a job back home? No, she handed in her notice. She couldn't take it anymore. She hated that job, it was destroying her, gnawing away at her insides with each passing day. Finally the day came when she'd had enough.

"You *quit*?" he says.

"Precisely." She took the plunge and went in to see the boss one morning, explaining that she'd had enough of office life, the flesh-colored carpets and the window frames stained brown, and so she handed in her notice.

"But how will you support yourself?" he asks anxiously.

"I have you," she says. For a moment he looks as horrified as she had hoped he would.

"*Me?*" he says.

"You're stable enough, aren't you?" she asks. "I thought you were the kind of man a person could lean on."

Fright seems to have arrested his face. "Well, yes, I am, but..."

She laughs and tells him not to worry. She has money.

"How much?" he asks.

"Enough so that I don't have to charge you for all the sex we're having," she says.

He coughs nervously. She says that she was only joking. She has plenty of money, it's more likely that he'll be the one sponging off of her. He insists that he's never done anything of the sort. Never sponged off a woman, never quit a job, never had money in the bank "just because." He says he comes from a line of farmers where, if you didn't want to work the land anymore, it would be unthinkable to leave that job without securing another first. She shrugs. Different folks, different strokes. Of course, if she ends up staying for a longer time, she'll have to do something, like take a career-oriented course or translate industrial manuals. She's always wanted to learn simultaneous interpreting anyway, and there are two schools for that in Florence. Okay, he says. Everything she's saying sounds good. She can stay with him for a while so she won't have to think about rent. That is if she wants to stay in Italy for a while, with him. If she takes care of dinner every night, they can call it even.

She walks around his attic apartment, which seems to her like heaven on earth. Two bathrooms, each with a shower. Tile roofs, the dome of Santa Maria del Fiore rising above all else, someone humming a tune down in the courtyard, flowers blazing in the neighbor's flower boxes. Chilling in the fridge is a bottle of white wine. The crowns of the pine trees in the courtyard stand in sharp relief against the sky, and at twilight the tang of burnt resin wafts through the open bedroom window.

IN THOSE EARLY days she walks around with a deep sense of satisfaction. As God created man, she creates this man. Perhaps that's why things will go so very wrong in the end, because she believes herself to be living in alignment with a narrative that has in fact never existed. Women do not create men, there are no such historical notions, no such legends. As for him, it soon becomes clear that his transformation keeps opening up new doors. Over dinner he takes pleasure in discussing the women who paid attention to him throughout the day. There was one woman who, when making herself a coffee at the machine outside his office, displayed her splendid bottom for him. How was he supposed keep his eyes on his work then? His laughter is genial; he is still so fat that when he laughs it appears genial. She can sense how much he'd like her to be laughing along with him, but she doesn't. He persists, wanting so badly for her to rejoice in this turn that his life has taken. He shows her a video of himself doing knuckle push-ups, rep after rep, with a big smile on his face.

"Who's filming you?" she asks.

"Giorgio," he says.

"I don't believe you," she says.

"I don't know what to say, it was Giorgio," he reiterates.

"A woman was filming you," she says.

"How can you tell?" he says.

"By your smile, you're trying to impress someone. You wouldn't smile like that at a man."

He stares at her awhile. "You're being paranoid," he says. "I thought you were the kind of person who'd be above it all, like a rose in a field of thistles. Turns out, you're a little prickly after all."

"Why don't you try being straight with me. Roses have thorns too, you know. Go on, tell me who was filming you."

The truth creeps out. A woman's name.

"How am I supposed keep a cool head while you're off at work?" she shouts.

She sees the astonishment, but also the answer, in his eyes. The answer is simple. The answer is that this is not about her keeping her cool. This is about his desire and the heights it can help him attain.

———

DAY TO DAY, despite the pain he has already begun to inflict on her, cohabitating with him is pleasant. He showers both morning and night, and drops his new shirts off at a laundry service so they stay spotless and crisp. He wears a nice cologne and moisturizes his head with a unisex lotion from a Spanish brand. Him being so neat and tidy now, she comes to think of him as *Il pulito*. She watches him closely and can find almost nothing about him that irritates her. She observes him, and he observes her. He tells her that she's so nice and quiet. Quiet as a mouse, he says, he's always wanted a woman who is as quiet as a mouse, a Minnie Mouse type who isn't intrusive.

"A *Minnie Mouse* type?"

"Yes, exactly. The name suits you. Is it all right if I call you Minnie?"

She shrugs. "If I'm Minnie, then you're Mickey, that goes without saying."

He looks in the mirror. "Mickey? Can't you pick something else?"

"Like what?"

"*Il toro? Il toro divino?*"

They laugh.

"Mickey will do," she says. "When you say 'intrusive,' how do you mean?"

Well, this is what's so nice about her, he says, she keeps her voice down and he can't really hear her going about her day in the apartment. Even when she opens and closes the doors and cupboards, she doesn't make a sound. Well, that's because she hates noise, she says. She hates noise and noisy people frighten her.

"A delicate princess," he says.

"A delicate princess? Hardly. I can use a drill and back up a trailer, so when you put it that way, it's insulting."

"But, Minnie, you can let yourself be weak with me. Strong women make us men weak. If we don't have the opportunity to demonstrate our strength, then what will we make of our masculinity?"

She considers what he's saying.

"Sure," she replies. "I'll gladly be a little weak with you. Now that you mention it, I can sense that I've wanted to be weak for a long time."

"You're perfect," he says. "Perfect for me."

This makes her happy, she takes it as a compliment, a compliment that bodes well. What she doesn't understand in the moment is that this compliment is also a request. A request that she continue to be perfect for him and not—if given the chance—mar the perfection he thinks he perceives. Instead her mind is occupied with thoughts of how to hide her flaws so that she can continue to be the person he says he perceives to be perfect. Deep down, of course, she knows, as does he, that perfection is a chimera. If she were forced to list each of her flaws and quirks, where would she even begin? As for her physical attributes, don't get her started, but when she puts on weight she goes soft and pasty, the fat expands around her waist and she becomes uniformly thick, like a cylinder, a marshmallow. If she spends too much time in the sun, her face turns red and swells up, her nose and cheeks get blotchy. Her hair has always been stiff and thick, more like a horse's mane than human hair. Just to mention a few. Then there's the occasional bout of social anxiety. This affliction puts her at odds in her home country, but it's an even worse fit in a Latin country where the social arena is where life plays out, where one must dare to stand up, speak up, and let the drama unfold around you. Had he been aware of it, he would have disapproved of her tendency to withdraw from the world and into herself, had he known that, back home, she sometimes wouldn't leave her apartment for days because she simply couldn't, and when she did, she'd go out at times when no one else was around. Why did she do this? She doesn't know. Another quirk, which surfaced in conjunction with the start of her studies to become a translator and the occasional stint as an interpreter, is that when she finds herself in stressful situations she has to recite everything going on inside her in more than one language. If she can't manage that, if there's a word she can't find, she can't move forward, can't think of anything else. She becomes paralyzed, because deep down she knows that if she resumes her task before finding the word, a curse might be activated. How did this come to be? She's not sure about this either, but she knows it to be true, and she also knows that the simple fact of having a thought can sometimes somehow give rise to a miniature reality of said thought, a reality that runs the risk of expanding and taking over one's own. This is another thing that Il pulito would have disapproved of, her belief in things with no rational explanation. It's not that she thinks about them all the time, but if she's being honest, yes, she does believe in things that have no rational explanation. With regard to her social anxiety and the belief that words can curse, she has read enough about psychology in self-help books to know that they could be considered neuroses. Neuroses can be mild and most people suffer from some form of neurosis, but a line is crossed when it becomes problematic to coexist with the neurosis, when the neurosis begins to constitute an obstacle in one's daily life. Do her neuroses constitute an obstacle in her daily life? She doesn't think so. After all, she's living her life, succeeding in most of what she sets out to do. Still, her neuroses can give rise to great unease and undermine her. She considered seeing a psychologist. But when she thought about all the people with real problems, people fleeing war or living in extreme poverty, she no longer felt entitled to her neuroses—as if they were afflictions among others that were the very mark of a delicate princess, and that's not what she wants to be. She has known shame, privilege, hypersensitivity, and she hates it, the way it all makes her feel sullied. Sullied by wealth and the bizarre spirit of the age, sullied by wealth and idiocy. Nature can be a balm. The trees draw out her heaviness and break it down inside them. But in Florence there is no nature. There are only bare hills, fenced-in vineyards, private hunting grounds, and city. The cypresses that can be seen in the distance beyond the city always belong to somebody. You can't go to them, you can't walk among them and inhale their scent or touch their trunks. They simply loom like a backdrop, a tableau, as solemn as they are unreachable. What will life in Florence be like for her in the long run, without the presence of genuine nature to absorb her afflictions? On the other hand, Florence is where Il pulito is, which confers an abundance of benefits that she really can't refuse.

IN THESE EARLY days they sometimes take his car out for an evening drive. She loves sitting beside him when he's at the wheel. They drive through tunnels in the mountains, out of Tuscany, and into Emilia-Romagna, past fields, old abandoned buildings that were once farms. Beautiful ocher farmhouses with olive groves, fig trees, and long tables in the garden. Balconies with views of the towns.

"Why has no one snapped these houses up and renovated them?" she asks.

He doesn't know. Why buy an old ruin when you can buy an apartment where everything is already taken care of? With a pool, an underground parking space, and air-conditioning. But the houses are in such a nice location. A bit isolated, according to him. He puts on some music, turns up the volume, and opens the sunroof, hot wind rushes in.

One evening they drive to an industrial area outside of Bologna. She laughs to herself. She's never been to a business park, not on a joyride. It would never have occurred to her to do so. But it occurs to Il pulito. He drives to the Fiat factory. They come to a stop in the parking lot and Il pulito turns off the engine. The setting sun meets the horizon and she watches as it lights up the sign above the factory. FIAT, it says, in big yellow letters set against the flaming sky.

"Imagine if I worked here," Il pulito says.

"What do you mean?" she asks.

"Imagine if I got the chance to work here," he reiterates.

She takes in the factory grounds.

"Would that be a good thing?" she asks. "Wouldn't it be a bit of a . . . nightmare?"

"Nightmare?" he says, looking at her with surprise. "Do you realize how many people want to work here?"

No, she doesn't.

"Work *here*," she says, "in a factory?"

"What world do you live in?" he says.

She falls silent. She looks at his profile as he gazes up at, as he *beholds*, the Fiat sign. It's as if he were seeing something tremendous. She takes her eyes off him so she can look at the sign as well, and tries to perceive its beauty. She tries to imagine a different kind of beauty, a kind of beauty to which she is not personally accustomed, but which surely exists and can be perceived, if one is so attuned.

"Imagine if I worked here," Il pulito continues dreamily. "Then I'd be driving around in a BMW."

"But if you work at Fiat, aren't you more likely to be driving a Fiat?" she asks.

It was meant as a joke, she can't really see Il pulito in a Fiat, he'd have to be stuffed in, squeezed in, what a ridiculous sight it would be, him driving around in that Fiat, such a big man in such a small car. But Il pulito doesn't appreciate her joke.

"Bosses drive BMWs," he says, starting the engine. "It's a law of nature."

Like bosses screwing their female employees is a law of nature, right? she wants to scream, because that's what you're up to, that's exactly what you're up to! But she doesn't scream. She sits in the passenger seat biting her tongue, and in the rearview mirror watches the Fiat sign fading into the dusk.

THERE IS A before and an after to the advent of manipulation. Suspicion finds its way in like damp through a plastered wall, cracking the facade at night as droplets expand into ice. Whatever it takes, she must get him to stay home, or to work from home. She tries to make the apartment as pleasant as can be. Wiping away thick layers of oily dust from kitchen surfaces and making elaborate lunches. Nonetheless he always excuses himself after lunch, he has to go, no, the issue can't be resolved remotely. She senses an acute interior sickness slowly setting in. It takes possession of her, it makes her suffer, but at the same time, when she lies down to rest, she might in her torpor be filled with curiosity about said sickness. It's as if she must explore it. Get acquainted with it, talk to it. When he isn't at home, she lies down for long periods just *sensing it*. She knows this is not healthy. But she can't help herself. It's like driving your cold fingers into hot mud, that's what getting acquainted with the sickness is like. The sickness is at once sweet and brutal, *dolce e bestiale allo stesso tempo, dulce y feroz al mismo tiempo*. A poison that tastes of sugar but is also corrosive. Sometimes she stays in bed even after he comes home at night. Dinner is no longer on the table when he walks through the door. She is in bed so often that she loses her appetite. He doesn't like this. She has to eat. One of his sisters had anorexia as a girl, and it left its mark on him, memories that weigh on him to this day. A faint smile crosses her lips when she hears this. So there's a chink in his armor, a chink through which something might find its way in?

"Aha," she says. "Tell me more."

He sits on the edge of the bed and shakes his shaved head. He doesn't want to. There are tears in his eyes. He's never talked about it with anyone. She lies there in silence, looking at him.

"But you have to talk about it," she says at last. "I can tell by looking at you, you're holding it in and it's eating away at you."

He nods.

"I want to," he says. "I do, but I don't know how to begin."

"Did you two look alike?"

"No, not at all. She was so beautiful. Before she got sick, she was the most beautiful girl in the neighborhood, maybe in all of Bari. Everyone was in love with her, everything seemed to grind to a halt when she walked by. And then she started losing weight. At first, it only made her more alluring. She became more fragile, brittle, it made you want to hug her and protect her. Then one day . . ."

"Yes?"

". . . you could see the corpse in her."

Il pulito tears up again. Soon he is weeping. The tears, large and lonely, roll down his cheeks.

"The corpse emerged with its dark sunken eyes, that wild

stare, the discolored whites of the eyes. A lifeless pale grayish gnarl appeared in her body. Her soft, round hips became angular, her heavy buttocks disappeared and in their place was a hollow sag. Her mouth became a dark hole, a silent cry for help in an endless throe of death. Her hair, which had been long, dark, and shiny, became tangled, lifeless, and ashen. She looked *frightful*. It was as if the dead had risen from the grave and had begun to wander the streets of Bari."

He has to take a break, because the words have amassed in his throat, are clogging it up. She too feels moved. Rarely has she seen men cry, and she could never have imagined that Il pulito, *il cazzone*, would be one of those few.

"I have one memory in particular," he continues despairingly, "and it is so awful, so shameful."

"Tell me," she says.

He shakes his head. "I can't," he says. "It hurts too much. I'm too ashamed."

"Speak from your heart, and the shame will go away. Shame is just the mildew that the soul spreads across things that have been sealed off, when in fact they need air to heal."

She touches his arm. It is a powerful arm. A tanned, masculine arm with a nice watch, a rolled-up sleeve, and dark hair. Are her fingers the first to touch this arm today? She doesn't ask. He swallows the lump in his throat, clears his throat.

"Okay," he says. "Okay, I'll give it a try."

"Take all the time you need. I like listening to you."

"Okay, Minnie, here goes. In those days I was working as a bodyguard for a local politician who would travel abroad for the summer, so then the whole staff would get a few weeks off. On the first Sunday of the vacation, the whole gang of us went to the beach. Five young men on a beach—needless to say we had high hopes of finding a bunch of girls. My sister was already very sick, but had started seeing a psychologist. Afterward I came to understand that the psychologist had encouraged her to not feel ashamed and to put herself out there even in her condition—an approach to treating this kind of disorder that was apparently in vogue at the time. So there we are in the sand, the whole crew. And she comes walking by. I see her the second she sets foot on the promenade, she's walking along like a shadow, but I pretend not to see her because I don't want her to come over to me and the others, we were on the lookout for a group of healthy girls, after all, I didn't want my colleagues to see that an illness like that runs in our family, I didn't want them to think of her whenever they looked at me from here on out, having a mental illness is not a good fit for jobs that require immediate strength and courage. But there she was, looking out across the beach. I'm keeping my eye on her as I lie down on my towel, trying to make sure she doesn't spot me. Suddenly I hear her shouting. Loud and clear, she's calling my name. I close my eyes and pretend to be asleep. The others don't seem to have heard, the roar of the sea drowns her out. My sister stops shouting. I slowly open my eyes and see her on the move. I'm afraid she'll come my way, but she doesn't. She walks to the middle of the beach, maybe fifty or sixty yards away from us. She unrolls her mat. And she takes off her tunic. She does it standing up, when she could just as well have done it sitting down. Why are you standing up, you dumb sick person, I thought. She stands there pulling off her tunic in the sun and sea breeze. Once her tunic is off, it's a gruesome sight. The whiteness of the corpse radiates from within. It's as clear as day: the corpse, the death radiating from her every pore. Her eyes are peering out of her skull. She looks around and notices that people have turned in her direction, and she smiles at them. She's *smiling*, do you understand? There's no smiling when you look like that! There are no smiling corpses! And it's not really a smile, either, but death's grin. It's as if all conversation has stopped and the only sound is the endless roaring of the waves. She adjusts the bikini strings on her nonexistent hips, tying them slowly and carefully with her bony fingers. Please lie down, I think, let this spectacle come to an end. But she doesn't. She doesn't even begin to lie down, she starts *walking*. Do you understand, Minnie, she starts *walking*. She walks to the shoreline and when her feet touch the water, she makes a quarter turn and continues along the water, in full glare, letting people gawp in horror. I think: This must be some absurd exercise that the psychologist insisted upon. I want to sink through the earth. By now the whole team has sat up and is staring at her too, but of course they don't know that she's my sister. What the hell is that . . . ? one of them says. Christ, what an eyesore, another says. The living dead, *una morta viva, cazzo, porca puttana,* says a third. I rest my cheek on the hot sand. The sensation of heat is magnified by my shame. For fuck's sake, I think, go home. Go home, just go home, the sick, the terminally ill shouldn't be wandering around on beaches where people are sunbathing and having a nice time. She does everything but. After she's walked back and forth a few times with everyone's eyes fixed on her, she finds a new place to sit. She—my sister, but also the corpse inside her—walks up to a *family*. She takes a seat only a few feet away from a mother nursing an infant under an umbrella. Two kids, around five, are sitting in front of her and a man who must be their dad. My sister takes a seat right there in the sand, looks at the woman nursing her child, and smiles. I see it, and I realize that she cannot possibly be aware of how grotesque she seems. It's part of the illness. You can't see what you actually look like, you are blind to your own shadow of death. The nursing woman seems to have frozen to ice in the sunshine. She stares at my sister for a long time. Then she jumps up, the baby still at her breast, and starts screaming. Get away! she screams. Get away from here, get away from my children, get away from my family! The man stands up, rushes over and puts his arm around his wife's shoulders, pulls her backward, and plants himself like a wall between her and my sister. As if my sister were infected with death and was about to infect them too. Please go away, the man tells her. I understand that you are sick, but still, I beg you, find somewhere else to be. There's a spot over there, you don't have to sit right here, where there are children. I see the smile slip from my sister's face. The skull stares blankly at the father of the young children. I have a right to sit here, she says at last. I may be sick, but I still have a right to sit here. I'm not contagious. What I have is not contagious. The man nods. He walks over to his wife and children and closes their umbrella. He folds their towels and picks up their clothes and toys from the sand. The wife looks on, clutching the baby to her chest. They move to the far end of the beach. And so do lots of others. In the end, an empty circle has taken shape around my sister. A shining empty radius, maybe five yards wide. She sits alone, gazing at the sea. It's like there's an iron lump in my throat. After a while I get up and go home. I'm pretty sure that my sister is standing in her empty circle, watching me go, but I don't turn around."

He is weeping as he recounts this story. It's the shame draining, the mildew being washed away. Beneath the shame is the raw pain with which she now has the opportunity to help, to shoulder the burden, and in this way get closer to him. She wants to share in this moment fully, to be a human being next to another human being, to go through what he is going through, to relieve this pain. She feels it so clearly—the memory of his sister still cuts deep. Even though she can feel this, she is not in fact able to access her compassion; that ability has already been compromised by her own pain. He is too strong, she is too weak, she cannot for a moment forget the power he has over her, the ease with which he could hurt her if he so chose. Instead of feeling pity, she registers coolly and strategically that Il pulito has a sore spot, which he has now revealed to her. She knows where it is, and she can poke it with her finger; she could control him simply by touching that spot. It's a manipulative and wicked thought. At the same time, it holds the sweet certainty of victory. She completely forgets to ask where his sister is today, if she's okay. Il pulito collects himself. He can tell what's going on.

He wipes his eyes and says, "I never want to talk about this again. I'm grateful to you for listening, but I never want to talk about this again."

She wants to scream out that she is not able to receive this gift from him as she should. Focusing on another person's pain is impossible once you've started to bleed like she has. She wants to say as much, but instead she sits on the edge of the bed, paralyzed. She even gets one last chance when he's standing in front of her, shoes on and hands on his hips, as if he expected her to say something, to behave decently, but she can't, she just sits there staring at his feet because she knows that anything she might say now would sound false and this wouldn't be lost on him. Finally he turns and walks off across the room. The door slams shut behind him.

THE NEXT NIGHT she tries to repair the damage by asking him to tell her something about his childhood.

"Didn't I do that yesterday," he says.

"What you told me yesterday wasn't about your childhood," she objects. "I mean something from when you were *really* little."

He runs his hand across his head and says he comes from a large family, four brothers and two sisters, a father who grew olives and a mother who caught small birds in traps that she set on a heath covered in broom shrubs. Then she'd toss them into the meat grinder whole—beak, claws, and all—and roll little meatballs that crunched between their teeth as they ate.

He falls silent.

"Is that all?"

"That's all."

"What are your siblings doing now?"

"Living their lives," he says, standing up. "Living their lives, not sweating the small stuff. Which is exactly what you and I should be doing, Minnie."

She wishes he'd ask about her childhood, but he doesn't.

HAD HE ASKED about her childhood, she would have had a thing or two to tell him. For instance, that she comes from a village where a girl was brutally murdered when she was young and that she grew up with a murderer living only a few miles from her childhood home. A half-hour walk through the woods. He lived in a small house, a damp little murderer's house, the paint peeling and its walls crowded by dark trees. What a story it could have been had she been allowed to tell it, a true one at that. The murderer in the woods and her skirting his house on her walks. It might also have explained a thing or two. The fear she sometimes felt around other people. Because she knows, unlike many others, what can hide behind a face. The murderer's face looked soft, as if swollen after soaking in water for a long time or as if it were made of sponges that had been run through a blender for hours. The murderer used to shop in the same country mart as her parents and sometimes she'd see him. He'd stand in line silently holding his goods in his arms. He had small, square glasses and a gaze that was heavy and dark, a gaze that was confined by those small glasses, as if his eyes needed an enclosure, a frame so that the evil in them would not find its way out, expand, and take over the world. The murderer's gaze would on occasion come to rest on her or her friends. A hush would descend upon them because they knew that they'd done something to attract his gaze, and there might be a punishment for that something, even if they did not understand how they were at fault or what that punishment might be. For many years no one knew that the murderer was the murderer, for many years it was believed that the perpetrator was some "outsider," someone who had been passing through, "perhaps a person or persons from the Continent." When it came to light that he was the malefactor, it seemed obvious and everyone said that they had sensed it. That man, such a recluse, sitting alone in his house in the woods, and those strange comments he'd make about violence and women when he went to parties. A recluse harboring a demon within. That's how she'd always explained it to herself. A recluse harboring a demon within, and when he took off his glasses his eyes became those of the demon. Often when she thinks of the murderer there in his house in the woods, she feels fully at ease because he is dead now. He hung himself with a sheet in prison. But the memory of him can still unleash in her a panicked fear. What would she have done if she'd fallen into his hands? If she had run into him while walking in the woods, if he had passed by while she was sitting alone in the old deserted car between his house and her parents', what would have happened if reality had slipped a few degrees, if everything had taken a slightly different turn? Might he have taken her to the house of murder, tortured her like he tortured the other girl? Certain screams can cut through the night and certain nights can reach into eternity.

But why is she thinking about all this now? Dark worn-out thoughts that she's been thinking for all these years but that never lead anywhere. Can't she simply live in the here and now? Living in the now is sometimes the only solution. And isn't Florence a beautiful city, isn't it the very opposite of her village, can't she muster a little gratitude, allow herself to live here with Il pulito and become a different person? She has to push away thoughts of the past, because if the past is given too much space, you drown in it. Everyone has their scars. Her move to Florence brings with it the opportunity to transform, to surgically remove a whole slab of scar tissue. This is how she should be thinking: Finally, an opportunity to transform and get rid of a whole slab of scar tissue.

SHE STAYS IN bed in the morning. The hot, sick mud inside makes her listless. She eats no breakfast. Il pulito brings her coffee and fruit on a plate, but all she does is shake her head. He slowly makes his way to work, but calls several times during the morning. This elicits in her a purring feline pleasure. He spends the afternoon at home. He sits next to her in bed and takes his meetings there, by phone. He asks her to take off her panties and lie on her side with one leg over the other, then rests his hand on her rump while she sleeps. She could have lain like that forever, and the world around them could have crumbled, but she would have stayed put, quietly and happily withering away under his warm hand as the grip inside her tightened and she became more and more entangled in desire. The less she eats, the more tired she gets, but it doesn't matter, because now she has his attention. Being strong and alert is overrated. If you're too strong, you end up carrying a heavier load, that goes without saying.

Then one afternoon she wakes up because a hunger inside her has been roused like a wild animal. It's as if it has suddenly come to life and is now rampaging through her guts. It impels her to do *whatever it takes* to find food. A primal force. He says he has to take care of a task at work, and for once she is not worried but grateful.

"Of course," she says. "I'll be here resting."

She listens as he changes his shirt, moisturizes his head, puts on his sneakers. Then he leaves. She gets up and goes to the window. There he goes, walking to his car. She pulls off her nightgown and puts on a dress. Then she walks down to the restaurant on their street, the one where the road workers eat their fatty cuts of meat and boiled gigantes during their lunch break. And so she orders, and eats. The bread in the bread basket, then the fatty meat and boiled vegetables; she asks for another portion, the cook comes out to take a look at her, asks where she's from and if all women from her country eat this much, but she doesn't care, just hand over the food she says, and eats it up, dessert too, and once she's polished all that off she wipes up the leftover panna cotta with the last piece of bread and washes it down with lashings of soda. Then she notices the road workers at the next table staring at her. She gets up and walks with her head held high to the counter while stifling a burp. She pays and sneaks back up to the apartment. There she lies on the bed like a bloated reptile, digesting. In the evening, Il pulito returns home. He has brought food. Fine and nicely selected sushi for her, but she gives her head a feeble shake.

"You have to eat," he says.

"Another day," she whispers.

"You're worrying me," he says.

She relishes this. She's jabbing a stick right into his sore spot.

All of a sudden he says, "Though today something strange happened. I'd forgotten some papers at home, and when I came back to get them, you weren't here. But when I walked back down the street, I saw you, Minnie, sitting in the restaurant downstairs. At first I didn't believe my eyes and I had to go back and check. But it was you, and you were eating like ..." He chuckles. "I had no idea a woman could eat like that. Not even my father would eat like that after working in the fields all day. I stood there for a long time, watching you, but you didn't see me. You were too consumed by the food."

She feels so ashamed her eyes might boil in their sockets. So he was standing there, watching her. He has seen right through her. With this, his sore spot has been sealed with cement; never again will she be able to get at it. She comes off like an idiot. With his honor-oriented southern mindset, she must come across like some hoity-toity Nordic fool.

"Now, now, Minnie Mouse," he says, stroking her hair, "wanting Mickey to think she's about to die ... Minnie, wanting Mickey's attention, wanting Mickey to stay home and take care of her ..."

Go, she thinks, because what can she possibly say. Leave me here to simmer in my shame in peace.

"But it doesn't actually matter," he whispers, "because I never really thought you were going to die." He strokes her hair again. "Your hair," he says. "Your hair tells me that you have what it takes to get through this. You don't have the hair of a dying person. Your hair tells me that you're not sick at all and one day you'll be able to get up, full of even more strength. You are going to live, Minnie."

She just lies there. He sits on the edge of the bed. She

hears him humming calmly and warmly. But then, when he thinks she has fallen asleep, he gets up and tiptoes to the door. She wants to fly at him like a giant bat and shout: Where are you going? Where are you going, who are you going to see, why am I not enough for you? But she keeps quiet. She knows she has to keep quiet and work on earning back his respect. She has to put up with more. Maybe she should even rack up a few little secrets of her own, as a kind of counterbalance.

Such are her thoughts.

HE GETS A little more heavy-handed, but it's still good over-all. He lifts her up more often, grabs her harder when he's turned on, sometimes he grabs hold of her hair and tugs. One night after she's had a few drinks, she says, "Can you promise not to break me to pieces?"

He laughs.

"For your own sake too," she continues. "I mean, that wouldn't be good for you, either."

He leans toward her, his dark eyes narrowed.

"Don't tell me what I can and can't do," he says. "You don't make my decisions for me. Maybe I need to break you apart so you grow whole again. Maybe I'm all that's holding you together. You can't possibly know nor are you supposed to. The only thing you need to know is that you must sur-render. If you don't put yourself in my hands, you'll rob me of my manhood, and then I won't want you anymore."

EVERYTHING IS ESCALATING quickly now. Inflections and insinuations build into full-blown arguments, which in turn degenerate into loud, dramatic brawls. On a few occasions, the neighbors bang on the wall, shouting, *Calm down, for God's sake, calm down!* This isn't happening, she thinks. I'm not the kind of person who gets the neighbors banging on the wall, I'm thoughtful, calm, and collected. But then she hears herself screaming and realizes that this is not in fact the case. Even her self-image is skewed; anorexia isn't a prerequisite for having a flawed sense of self. She searches for an explanation. The explanation lies in desire. Lust and aggression can be related, can trigger each other, and sometimes all that separates the two is a thin membrane. This is what's happening to her: Things are merging. Some types of sexuality are, of course, transgressive. If, as a woman, you crave that kind of sexuality, you can't then request for it to be shut off at a particular moment. That's not how men operate. A man is not a keypad or an instrument board, there is no Stop button. That's why certain situations shouldn't be entered into, because certain situations can only lead to a meltdown, after the process of overheating reaches a point of no return. Not to mention, a person's sexuality extends beyond the bedroom. It is a kind of keynote, a sound that can be heard in other rooms as well. His sexuality is stronger than hers. She can sense it. He is her superior in this, and she hates herself for the pleasure her inferior position accords her. If only she could trust him. If she could trust him, surrendering to him would have been easier. But situations arise from which she cannot extricate herself. He should bear that in mind, he should be enough of a man to create a safe space for her and make sure its retaining walls hold. Had he done so, she might have felt calmer, freer. Now she feels unsafe and must reassure herself of obvious truths again and again. Such as: Sexual games aren't harmful as long as you aren't harming anyone. Adults having sex, nothing harmful in that. That's how she tends to think. He uses these games to spice things up, and sometimes he wants to imagine her with other men. No harm done, right? After all, he's not actually asking her to do it, he's not putting their relationship in jeopardy by asking her to fool around with someone else, and in that sense his fantasies are purely innocent.

In the heat of the moment, he might say, "Tell me about the time you had sex with your boss."

"But I've never had sex with my boss."

"That doesn't matter, talk to me *as if* you had."

"Feels a little weird, since he wasn't my type at all."

She thinks of her former boss. A prankster with a briefcase and a bit of a mincing gait. Married to a woman called Gunnel. He had dandruff and a near ever-present dusting of it, like powdery snow, on his shoulders.

"Just do it, Minnie."

"I mean," she says, "I really wasn't attracted to him."

"Okay, but who cares, just tell me about the time you had sex with him. Pretend, damn it, Minnie, pretend he was someone else, be a little generous with yourself."

Okay, she's imagining that her boss was someone else. A more appetizing person. She fumbles her way toward a fantasy. How one thing led to the next, how they ended up in bed, she, the boss, and one of his colleagues. She senses his arousal, and his arousal is catching. More details, he wants details, and this isn't actually a problem for her, she can cobble together a story fairly easily, she can read his wants and desires and she can spin a story that causes stars to light up all through the dome of Il pulito's skull and sets his body aflame, and she does it because she wants to make him happy, she wants them to have the best sex he's ever had, she wants to be the best for him, and that's why she abandons herself and pretends she's someone else, someone who has sex with her boss every day, the boss and the boss's pal, every day and everywhere, at the office, on the desk, in the car, in hotels, in restaurants after closing time while a waiter goes about his business . . .

"Wonderful," he says stretched out on the bed, catching his breath. "Wonderful."

But later, as they're strolling through Florence in the evening sun, he says, "You know, Minnie, the thing with your boss, I wouldn't have thought that about you."

"What?"

"I didn't think you'd be one to fuck around like that."

"But, Mickey, I'm not! I never have been. I never did. You asked me to—"

"Don't play coy with me. Some of the things you talked

about must come from experience, there are some things that can't be imagined, can't be made up."

"Mickey, listen. I can, it's a little gift of mine, I can describe things as if I've been there, it's easy for me, ask me to do it now and I'll show you."

"*Can't bullshit a bullshitter*, Minnie," he says in English.

"Mickey. I'm not like that. I don't want to be that kind of person, I'm not as damn horny as you seem to think I am either, I'm just a completely normal person."

"You? A completely normal person? *Ma dai*, Minnie, *per favore!*"

She feels dirty. She makes a promise to herself to never, never ever, treat Il pulito to another fantasy. Silence will reign between them. Silence and stiffness, like an evening in southern Italy in a windowless house, a dull place where desire is kept in check. This is the only way to get him to respect her.

AT WHAT POINT does it all go off the rails? In a few weeks she will try to chart the sequence of events, try to pinpoint the moment the compass stopped pointing north. And as she goes about this task, despite her miserable state, she will smile as she remembers the first flush of joy. She will remember how in the beginning Il pulito had warmed the deep-frozen earth inside her, how he had thawed her, like the spring sun above winter's garden. When you, as a human being, experience something like this you rejoice in your own flourishing, in being blessed with access to the mysteries of the flesh—being given the chance to take shape, to grow from another person's soil, to be in the midst of the warming light that just keeps shining upon you. That is, until the fear arrives. The fear that the light will disappear, that it will shine on another body, that another woman will experience the joy that belongs to her. She can't stand the thought. As much as she wishes she could, she can't stand the thought that he knows more about other women's bodies than they do, just like he knows more about her body than she does. This disadvantage is too crushing for her to bear. She cannot accept the idea that another woman is getting to experience what she is experiencing with him.

"And how does your famed sisterhood fit into all this?" he asks with a smirk.

She can't answer, can't even pretend to smile. She tries to bat the thought away again, but can't. She becomes burdensome. As much as she doesn't want to be, she becomes obsessed, and burdensome. She has to have him all to herself. This is the abyss. Ownership is the abyss. As soon as the desire to own comes into play, you have to back off, accept that Il pulito belongs to a different weight class, and all the things you think you need aren't necessarily meant for you. That's when you have to take a step back. But she cannot. Even though he very politely asks her to back off. Even though he, with great calm, explains to her that she must not believe that she owns him. However much he likes her, he can't cut off his cock and tie it up in a pink silk bow for her. She can't be left to swan around town with his cock dangling from a pink bow, like womanhood's ultimate trophy. She has to respect him for who he is. No, no, it's not possible. If he wants to be with her, he has to show her respect. She's monogamous, he has to be too. With controlled rage in his voice he says that she *has to* stop. Do what Latin women do, turn a blind eye or find a jolly of her own. *A jolly of her own?* Is he insane? He says it again: She can't be like this.

"Back off," he says, with a darkened gaze. "Back off."

For a moment, she can picture her healthy side taking the lead: getting up, taking her packed bag, and checking into a hotel. But in reality she stays put, thinking there must be a way. There must be a way for him to be hers and hers alone. She doesn't know how, but there must be a way.

THEY'RE LYING IN bed. The door to the balcony is open. She's reading Jung, he's reading Grisham. It's quiet in the apartment, and when she glances up from her book she sees motes of dust slowly sailing through the last rays of the afternoon sun. She hopes the neighbors are at home. So they can hear how calm they are, how peaceful it *actually* is between them. Suddenly she reads a few lines that seem to be speaking directly to her, to them. She asks Il pulito if he wants to hear. He sighs.

"Is it from that psychologist?"

"Yes, it is. Are you up for it?"

He says sure, he'll listen. She reads: "*Spirituality and sexuality are not your qualities, not things which ye possess and contain. But they possess and contain you; for they are powerful daemons, manifestations of the gods, and are, therefore, things which reach beyond you, existing in themselves.*"

He lets out another sigh. "And?"

"And?"

"Yes, and?"

"You really don't get it, do you? You don't see the

connection? You don't see that we, you and I, are embedded in these lines?"

He laughs. "The way you put two and two together, Minnie!"

"But don't you understand?"

"No, I don't understand. Not this. What I do understand is that you should be reading a different book."

He holds up the Grisham novel, says she can have it when he's done. He goes back to his reading. She lies there in silence, looking outside. The sky has turned red. A few lone clouds seem to be floating by, but otherwise it has turned orange-red, as if the ocher from the tile roofs has stained the sky.

"Look at the sky," she says. "It looks like it's bleeding."

"Read a different book, Minnie," he mutters without looking up. "Just read a different book, and I'm sure everything will sort itself out."

THE FIRST TIME a situation truly erupts, he puts his hand on her throat and presses down. She whispers, *No no no, don't kill me.* Then he laughs. He has a black belt in karate, he spent a decade as a bodyguard, he was born in Bari and spent years living in Algiers, doesn't she think he knows exactly where the line is so she doesn't have to worry about *dying*?

"*Figuriamoci,*" he says, "as if I don't know when I'm killing someone and when I'm not."

She has to *trust* him. He bends her head over the edge of the bed and presses.

"*Now* I'm killing you," he says. "*This* is what that feels like."

Again she tries to whisper a plea for him to stop but can't get the words out. She manages to keep her cool though, thinking that in this moment he is being driven by something ancient, something animal. If you meet a predator in the woods and start running, the animal will automatically chase after you. Something inside the animal gets unleashed. But if you stand still then slowly back away, you have a chance. She reins in her panic and lies perfectly still, goes so far as to shut her eyes. He lets go. Only then does she notice that she has peed herself. The sight of the urine horrifies him. He jumps up and plants himself in the middle of the room. He stands there, looking at her sitting in the spread of wetness. She is so ashamed that her eyes tear up, and the shame keeps creeping through her until she has turned bloodred.

"Don't look at me," she mutters. "Not now, not like this."

"I'm sorry," he shouts. "I'm sorry, I'm sorry, I'm sorry!"

She gets up, takes off her panties and bra, and rushes into bathroom. Her thighs are wet and her body is still burning red with shame. Meanwhile, he puts her underwear and sheets in the washing machine. She thinks she hears him sobbing but doesn't trust her ears. The mattress is put out to air on the balcony, but the biting renal stench does not dissipate, and as they are about to drift off to sleep it appears, like a vapor, a memento of the day that was.

"Have you forgiven me?" he whispers.

"Go to sleep," she replies.

This city, she thinks before she falls asleep, and then the smell of urine and the two of them whose insides are disfiguring with such speed. As if there were a monstrous version of each of them, into which they were now turning. She wants to cry, release some kind of sadness, but can't get a grip on the feeling.

Later that night, a bat flies into the bedroom. It is an exceptionally hot night, and perhaps, she thinks, it was the heat that caused Il pulito to lose his temper earlier in the day. She thinks the apartment at night has begun to smell like a Finnish smoke sauna, burnt wood atop a strong base note of salmiac. The bat flits despairingly along the wooden ceiling in the darkness. She knows bats symbolize death, but in symbology death isn't always negative. Death suggests an ending, and an ending implies the birth of something else. What could it be? Have they reached the end of the road because of this event, and a reversal is now about to take place? Suddenly the bat flies so close to her face that she can feel the draft from its wings. Startled, she sits up and turns on the lamp.

"You have to get the bat out," she says. "*Il pipistrello*. It's a funny word. *Murciélago* in Spanish, *pipistrello* in Italian, *chauve-souris* in French, *bat* in English, *fladdermus* in Swedish. It's one of those words that doesn't connect with itself in any way."

He looks at her, dazed and uncomprehending.

"You're giving me a vocabulary lesson *at a time like this*?" he says.

"I'm just saying—"

"I'll make sure it gets out," he says. "Mickey will take care of everything, you can rest easy."

When she sees his bare back under the open skylight she thinks he looks lonely, and that there's probably a lot of good in him in spite of it all.

SHE HAS NO friends. No one she can call, no one she can confide in. When did that happen? When did she become "friendless"? She must have had friends at some point? She remembers the feeling, and when she does, it's as if she can hear conversations in the distance, through time and space, friendly conversations that in some dimension are still ongoing. Secrets, interest, understanding, warmth, generosity. But in the present she bears it all alone, because it's simpler that way. She doesn't want to go out and make some beautiful female friend here in Florence only to introduce her to Il pulito and watch him eye the woman up, his way of receiving her with measure but also desire. By now she has his number. Another option would have been to find an ugly friend in Florence. But even this does not appeal to her. Why? To be honest, completely honest, it's because she doesn't have it in her to account for what's going on. To stand there, feeling ashamed of herself. Her moldering soul. A friend would have looked at her with an unvarnished gaze. A friend would have told her that she is on the wrong path, that the path she has chosen leads nowhere, and if it does lead anywhere, it's straight down to hell. And this is precisely what she cannot bear to hear. This is a problem. It is, it's absolutely a problem that the path she's on is leading straight to hell, and it's a problem that she doesn't have anyone around who can bring her to her senses.

But those are only two of her many problems, and they seem to her, as deplorable as this may sound, to be far from the worst among them.

THEY'RE GOING TO meet up at five o'clock on Piazza della Santissima Annunziata. At two o'clock she leaves the apartment. She goes shopping in the city center. Benetton and Promod, she'll find things there. She wants to be the best version of herself when she meets Il pulito tonight. She wants him to be proud of her. Italian men love feeling proud of their women. She tries some things on and then some more. Nothing fits right. Her trousers don't have a nice fall, it's all weird, her face looks tense and unhappy. In the end she buys a pair of dark blue ankle-length trousers and a striped T-shirt, goes into a bar and changes in the restroom, stuffs the old clothes into her handbag. Il pulito doesn't even notice her new outfit. He's distracted, sitting in the evening sun, thinking about something he doesn't want to share with her. They drink prosecco. Her trousers strain at the thigh and the sweat in her armpits lingers cold.

Being a man, she thinks as she watches him sitting there, is like living in Guatemala. No seasons, no cycles, no swings—just sun and stasis in the body, seventy-seven degrees all year round. Being a man is like being a stowaway on the upper deck and simply enjoying the view. As for a woman, she's struggling in the Arctic on a sputtering ship, its engines threatening to deadlock any second now, all the while she hopes that an iceberg won't block her progress so she can keep sailing along for another few sea miles at a decent speed.

From where she's sitting in the evening sun, she also realizes that she is no longer *choosing* him but is *stricken* with him. Had she been able to leave him, she would have done so right now. But she can't. She's caught in something, some kind of grip that won't let go. Maybe she should just let herself be crushed. Stop struggling and let herself be crushed without putting up a fight. This insight provides immediate relief. An ancient piece of wisdom that modern times have kept hidden from her. Modern times dictate that no one, not man, not anyone else, whomever they may be, has the right to crush woman. But there is a much older and deeper narrative, where woman is in fact constantly being crushed, and that's pretty much all there is to it. It's an awful narrative, she thinks, a narrative that doesn't benefit her in the slightest, but time is indifferent to what she as an individual thinks is awful. Besides, who *isn't* suffering? To escape suffering would be an unnatural privilege and why should she be the first in the history of the world to be accorded this privilege? How arrogant it would be to be persuaded of such a thing. Yes, the insight undeniably comes as a relief. Why has she resisted at all? she wonders. This is a matter of her fate. She has been assigned no spectacular task. The cosmos doesn't give a damn, the cosmos is chillingly neutral. She will be crushed by him, go under for him. In that, at least, she will be pure, as pure as ash among the flames. She belongs to a branch of womanhood that is not representative of civilization, a branch where self-respect has not taken hold, a branch that does not feel indignation, that enters into situations that a slightly smarter woman never would. She is an offshoot, an aberration. There is no true love in her, there is only brutish, bovine stupidity. She despises herself. She wants to be somebody else. Not just anyone else but definitely somebody else. Why is she thinking these thoughts? How much wine has she had?

The wind stirs her hair and she feels his hand on her head.

"It's time to go home," he says.

The evening air is peculiar and a bit cold as they walk through the city.

As if in collusion with their story.

SHE HAS PAID a few visits to the pharmacy in Il pulito's neighborhood. To buy aspirin, toner, and picking up Il pulito's blood pressure medication, like he asks her to. The woman at the register starts to recognize her. With each visit, the woman becomes chattier and chattier. She's not sure she likes it. Familiarity can be nice, but it has its drawbacks. The day will come when she and Il pulito will visit the pharmacy together and he'll do something strange, speak too loudly or stare too hard at some beautiful girl, and after that the woman's attitude toward her will change, there will be a streak of contempt and coldness in her voice. That's why she keeps her guard up, because she couldn't handle that shift, she'd rather do without the friendliness from the start.

One day she buys an oil for her intimate area. While the woman is ringing her up she says en passant that you get drier and drier with time.

"I'm only thirty-two," she says.

The woman chuckles. "Then you're on the brink."

"Of what?"

"The abyss."

She stares at the woman, unsure of what to say. The woman seems amused by her unease.

"When I was young it used to smell like freshly baked bread in my armpits and between my legs," she says. "My husband *loved* it. Now I smell like nothing at all, and he's met someone else." The woman holds out the bag. "And that was that. So you know. *Arrivederci.*"

She takes the bag without a word. A seed of panicked fear has begun to sprout inside her. To dry up, to let blood. On the way home she tries to tell herself that she is a very aquatic woman, she will never dry up. There must be women who never do. But this is also when she realizes that growing old with Il pulito is an impossibility because she cannot imagine him being confronted with *any* age-related defect. To face him she must rally every perfection she can, and something as devastating as old age is out of the question between them.

Later that evening she asks his opinion of her bodily fluids. He smiles at her.

"I love everything about you because you let me do what I want."

"Let?" she says. "You help yourself."

"Yes," he says. "But there's resistance and then there's resistance. As a man you have to be able to tell the difference, otherwise you risk putting a foot wrong."

"What do you mean?"

"With you, Minnie, I never have any doubts."

She casts her eyes down. The conversation went wrong, as it often does with Il pulito. You plot a course, but then he flies at you like a baseball bat, whacking you so hard you have no choice but to go another way, toward an unknown destination, previously unimaginable. She says as much. He laughs.

"Trust me," he says. "I'm not going to hurt you. There's nothing wrong with your bodily fluids. And besides, it's what's happening inside you, in your brain, that I love most of all."

The fear inside her keeps growing. The pharmacist has brought her around to the idea that one day, soon or in the future, she will notice that a veil of boredom will have been drawn over his gaze. When her body has dried up and every scenario in her mind has been played out, he won't desire her anymore. She cannot imagine Il pulito absent his desire for her, it is as if there can be no such version of him. They will never be able to share other dimensions. Never will they walk in the woods together, never read the same books, or be part of the same social circle. When her body dries up it will all be over. What will I do then? she wonders. Then she remembers that suicide is always an option, and the thought provides sudden relief.

ONE NIGHT SHE wakes up in bed and can't fall back asleep. He lies next to her, breathing heavily. He has kicked off the sheets, leaving his naked body open for observation. She knows most of it well, but when she sees his feet she realizes that she has never taken a proper look at his toes. Quietly she sits up. His toes are long, pale, and sturdy. But what distinguishes them most is that they are a bit crooked, angled in different directions on either foot, as if they were sea grass underwater, sea grass being swayed by a current that has stopped mid-flow. They don't quite seem to belong to a human being, but to something else. A prehistoric creature, a creature endowed with a higher dose of libido and aggression from birth, a creature that does not fit into modern times and has therefore painstakingly adapted its entire appearance to the parameters of the outside world, that has squeezed its flesh into a suit but has kept its toes as a hidden testimony to its inner essence. A kind of tenderness rises through her. Suddenly Il pulito looks so defenseless with those unusual toes pointing this way and that. She wants to stroke them, feel his defects against her skin, embrace them, but stops herself.

If he wakes up to her touching his toes, he won't understand, and if she tried to explain it by talking about prehistory, defects, and tenderness, he'd only think she was even weirder than he already does. Another factor to her disadvantage.

Instead she lies down and takes a book from the stack she brought from home and placed at her bedside. She turns to a random page of *Dark Spring* by Unica Zürn. She reads, not without a little shudder: *One is always exposed to dangers. Both of them are aware of that. And yet such dangers promise a perverse temptation—like a deliverance from the monotony of the everyday, the yawning abyss of boredom.*

SHE LOVES THESE mornings. The clean, cool air flowing into the apartment, the sight of the church domes and the mountains in the distance, the promise of a fresh start, the chance to do everything differently. He comes out of the shower and puts on cologne, moisturizes his shaved head, all the while looking at her darkly. His eyes say: *I'm warning you, don't do anything stupid.* She doesn't do anything stupid. She simply lowers her eyes and doesn't smile back. She knows the effect this has. It's what triggers him the most, her being harsh and coolly dismissive rather than accommodating. It's the chase, he once said. I have to be allowed the chase. I want to feel that a trophy is something I've won, not something being handed to me because then it has no flavor. I'm not a scavenger, I'm a hunter.

Contempt has an excellent effect on a hunter. He'll slowly stalk after her. She says, "What do you want?"

"Nothing," he replies.

"Lucky for you," she says and makes her way to the kitchen.

"Lucky for me how?" he asks from behind her.

"Lucky for you that you don't want anything, because if you did, you wouldn't get it. You're too old, too ugly, and I can do so much better than you."

On some occasions he lets a comment like this slide, and those are occasions on which he has plans with someone else later in the day. That's when he lets it slide, and might even laugh a little. It's the starting shot for her anxiety, no, it's the starting shot for her nightmare. *Incubo, pesadilla, cauchemar.* If cheating isn't on his calendar, this will be the starting shot for his lust. He'll entice her with a mixture of nagging and gentle violence. It's irresistible. He speaks directly to her body, to her flesh. Her soul might be screaming for her to run, to take to her heels and flee, but the flesh does not heed the soul. The flesh goes its own way, and since it is the flesh that is material, the soul can but follow along.

When it is over, she always feels a sense of loss. As if she had been walking around her inner rooms in dirty shoes. A faint tug in the left pectoral muscle. She loses a part of her soul each time she lets her flesh decide. This is the price of passion. The wearing away of the soul. Dignity wearing away, decency, all that is self, one's inner core, withering. Only the flesh thrives. And if the flesh comes to harm, it heals quickly and is soon fit for another round.

Before her degeneration begins in earnest, he is so fundamentally secure in his manhood that none of her insults can touch him. He might agree that yes, true, he is a weak man with a small good-for-nothing member. Only a man who doubts nothing about himself can say a thing like that. This she understands. It's partly a consequence of her fortifying him, according him some of her own power, but it's also because deep inside, deepest down, he knows what he is. But in time, this too changes. He undermines her, but she undermines him as well. After some time she can't say anything condescending about his manhood without it being like flicking a lit match into a sea of gasoline. After some time he loses his stamina. He drives himself into the ground. His pulse, blood pressure, and obesity take their toll on his potency. The worse his potency gets, the sorer a point this becomes. Eventually he can't even brush up against it without screaming out in a wild rage. A puff of wind on his potency, and every part of him aches, every fiber of his ego roars in pain. His manhood is the totem around which their entire relationship revolves. It's the underlying agreement that doesn't even need to be articulated because it's so self-evident. His manhood is to be preserved and protected. Praised, even. *You must worship his dick.* A friend once gave her this advice. A feminist friend, it must be said. The friend talked at length about women's struggles and men's difficult-to-manage personalities, went so far as to say that all men were potential rapists, and she had almost stopped listening when the friend suddenly pivoted and got to the heart of the matter. The heart of the matter was that, all that being said, there is a single underlying truth: "If you really want a good relationship with a man, you have to worship his dick." Sort of shocking advice, considering the friend's feminist stance. But still waters run deep. Yes, they do. And the advice was useful, in any case. She has found that it works. She was always able to joke around with him when the "worship principle" was fundamental to their relationship. But when the trust started to erode, when she stopped *worshipping*, everything became more difficult. Joking around is fine, as long as it's not taken too far. It's a matter of knowing where the line is. She knows where the line is. The times she crosses it are not because she doesn't know where it is but because she's so angry with him that she turns him into a pig and in doing so makes him hate himself as well. Being beaten is part of the bargain, but sometimes it's worth it.

"That's what Circe did. She turned Odysseus's men into pigs."

"Circe?" he says when she brings her up.

He hasn't read Homer. He thinks Circe is Cersei in *Game of Thrones* and doesn't see what she has to do with their relationship.

She laughs. But she can only look down her nose at him for brief spells.

He is forever crushing her.

She walks by his side through Florence, experiencing how he is in collusion with womanhood, and this is all it takes for her to be turned into a nobody.

ONE EVENING SHE is given the opportunity to tell him about the horrific murder in her hometown. But nothing turns out as she had hoped. They're about to start watching a TV series. The series begins with a dead, naked woman bound to a tree.

"So this is the opening scene?" she says in a measured tone.

"Yes," he replies.

She explains to him that because she grew up in a village where a girl was brutally murdered, she does not watch films or series that revolve around brutally murdered women.

"If a narrative has to be built around that," she says, "then I don't want to see it."

"*Narrative?*" he says. "Can't you just say 'series' like the rest of humanity?"

"There are a lot of other things that I can watch," she says. "Zombies. We can watch a zombie series."

"Don't you mean a *zombie narrative*? With no brutally murdered women?"

He jeers. Says that this is what he wants to watch. He's heard it's good. He's sorry that she comes from a village where a girl was murdered, but that kind of thing happens all over the place and everyone at the office is talking about this series. She suggests they go for a drive instead. To the Fiat factory in Emilia-Romagna? He shakes his head. He's watching this series. If that's the case, she says, she's going to read in bed. He laughs dryly.

"Minnie," he says, "I know exactly what you'll be like in a few years. One of those gray feminists you see around sometimes, who smells of old books and musty wool cardigans and who hasn't had sex in years."

"Shut up," she says.

He shuts up. She goes to bed but doesn't fall asleep; she listens to him binge-watching into the small hours. Every now and then he gets up and goes, humming, into the kitchen to refill his glass with port. Old Invalid, if she remembers right. His brand of port is Old Invalid. She chuckles to herself. But she cannot fall asleep, so she lies awake, staring out into the night with the sound of the murder series in the background.

ONE DAY SHE strikes out on her own and goes to one of the interpreting schools. A seven-month course in simultaneous interpreting is offered there, not as expensive as she'd feared, and which practically guarantees work when she is done.

"There are many companies in the textile industry in this part of Tuscany," says the woman at the office. "You'll have assignments every day."

She thinks that this might be a good solution, a way of injecting a dose of normalcy into their relationship. If she also leaves the house in the morning, then perhaps some sort of equilibrium might arise. A normal life, instead of one where her days are spent in bed in the haze of an inner malady. However, they do want to test her language skills, because they've had problems with students who are non-native Italian speakers; simultaneous interpretation is difficult for them. She tries her absolute hardest and passes the tests. In the evening, she tells Il pulito, hoping that he will appreciate her accomplishment, feel a little proud of her for actually getting in even though she is not a native Italian speaker. But all he does is sit there, looking at her.

"Aren't you happy for me?" she says.

"I just don't understand what you want to achieve, Minnie."

"I want to earn a little money."

"I thought you had money."

"It's running out."

"You made it sound like you had plenty."

"Yes, but I'm saying that it's starting to run out."

He shrugs. "You can live off me. We can stop eating out and stay home more often."

She sees the danger in this. The darkness that would close in around them, the city that would become distant, the two of them alone at home most of the time. Her longing, his power.

"I'm doing this," she says resolutely. "Say what you like, but I can't spend the rest of my life sitting around waiting for you. You don't want to feel like I'm leeching off you either, do you?"

Eyebrows raised, he nods as if he were thinking "Indeed."

"Are there a lot of men there?" he then asks.

"Where?"

"At the school."

She looks at him with surprise. *A lot of men?* Then she understands and laughs. He's worried that she'll meet someone else. This pleases her somewhat. She takes it as a sign of affection, proof that he doesn't want to lose her. She doesn't think, as in retrospect she should have, that people only know others through themselves, so if you're worried that your partner will take up with someone else while you're not around, then you're likely to do the same. That's how it is: You know others through yourself and so the thief thinks that everyone is a thief, *piensa el ladrón que todos son de su condición*. But she does not see this now. Instead she winks at him and says that simultaneous interpreting requires *simultaneous capacity*. That is to say: no men.

He smiles wanly, points at her, and nods, as if she were an unbelievable nerd who actually has a point.

"I'll come with you," he says, "and see for myself what sort of place it is."

IL PULITO ACCOMPANIES her to the school. He walks quickly and quietly, holding her hand all the way up the stairs and into the classroom. There sit twelve women, all smiling kindly as they enter. Il pulito blooms, tells everyone that he's glad his *ragazza* is about to make a lot of friends and he hopes to see them all at their place some evening, he can treat them to prosecco and pasta with *radicchio e fave*. She is ashamed, as one is ashamed of a parent, and whispers in his ear that it's time for him to go.

"And now she's driving me away," he says and the women laugh, "so I'm off, or it'll be the end of me tonight, see you later, take care of my Minnie, *mi raccomando!*"

So he's off. The women keep smiling at her but she doesn't know what to say and in her embarrassment forgets to smile back.

ONE DAY, HOWEVER, she does meet a man. Not at the school, mind you, but no matter. It's on an evening when Il pulito won't be at home because he has a meeting that will run late. A large French train manufacturer has taken an interest in his company's products, and he has to take the visiting Frenchmen out to dinner afterward and "show off the best side of Florence." He promises to come home as soon as he can. At first she wants to demand proof. What kind of manufacturer is it, can he produce an email to substantiate his claim, proving that there is indeed one such manufacturer, an interest in the products, and a meeting? But then she reconsiders. Rationally speaking, such behavior would be absurd and furthermore she has decided not to feed her paranoia. She is supposed to be demonstrating self-control, earning his respect. So she simply says, "Good luck. I hope it goes well and you get some business out of it."

He smiles gratefully and disappears. In that hot apartment the afternoon feels interminable to her. No text messages from him arrive and the silence in the rooms is deafening. She decides to go to Esselunga supermarket and buy a box of sushi to eat on a bench in the park. She'll sit there, watching people go by, take off her shoes, basking in the evening air with her toes in the grass. The man in question is sitting on the bench right across from hers. She squints in his direction while eating her sushi with chopsticks, he squints back. She swings her foot a little, thinking that Il pulito is probably having dinner surrounded by some beautiful female colleagues right now, so she might as well sit here exchanging a few glances, altogether harmless, if one were inclined to compare. The man shuts his eyes and sits there like that—face turned to the evening breeze coming from the surrounding mountains. But he must sense her looking at him because eventually he opens his eyes, looks at her with a smile, and asks if she's from Florence or is she a tourist? He's from the United States. Nice, she thinks, finally a person from a civilized place in this modern world.

"I've seen you before, with a bald man," he says. "You live around here, in the neighborhood, right?"

"Yes, that's the primeval beast who's holding me captive," she says.

They both laugh. She feels uplifted but knows she's on thin ice. She's about to be unfaithful, she's debasing her partner, and she knows nothing about this man. Things can get dangerous very quickly when you put yourself out there, when you give in to this kind of cogwheel mechanism. She proceeds anyway.

"What's your name?" he asks.

She says her name is nothing special, but he can call her Minnie.

"Minnie?" he says. "How odd."

As for him, his name is Ben. A moment later they're walking to his apartment. This is *very* irresponsible, she thinks. I'm about to be unfaithful with a strange man. She is ashamed of herself, but not enough to refrain. If this is what Il pulito does, Minnie should too. She doesn't enjoy intercourse with Ben and makes sure he uses protection. At least she won't get pregnant or contract a disease. What does Il pulito do when he's unfaithful? Does he protect himself? He's a hygienic person, she thinks, and draws the reassuring conclusion that he always uses protection when he is being unfaithful.

OUT OF SHEER boredom, she sits in the park the next day too. And the next and the next. Ben shows up every afternoon. A routine takes shape. It's a bit of a toss-up with the condom in the end, it's so much nicer without one, and he experiences a different kind of pleasure altogether, it's quite wonderful actually. But she can't relax, because if Il pulito finds out, he'll kill her. Ben asks about him. She answers evasively. Ben says that if things with Il pulito were good, she wouldn't be sitting here with him now. She knows Ben is looking down on her. She is being unfaithful. He dreams of a faithful woman and she's already proven herself unworthy. She believes this to be the case, she can sense his judgment. By the way, the topic of fidelity has never come up, so who's to say that he doesn't already have a faithful woman back home in New Orleans?

THE SICKNESS KEEPS spreading, almost all of her is now overcast and heavy. She remembers having been a completely different person. A person who had other things on her mind, such as nature, horses and forest walks, poems and novels. Very rarely sex. Back then she had a dandruffy boss for whom she felt no attraction and that was fine, all was as it should be, they did their work, fulfilled their obligations, their everyday functioning lives were boring. Under the circumstances, she was healthy. Now, however, it's as if her brain has been inflamed by this interior sickness. The soft, hot mud. Sex is ever-present, and sexual thoughts drag with them debris, like a trawler dredging up a mass of dead, half-rotten, hidden things from the bottom of a lake. She becomes even more critical of herself. The icy eyes of self-examination, as the great woman writer from her country once wrote. Part of the problem, she thinks, is that she doesn't know who her competition is. She would have needed to *see* Il pulito's other women in order to assess the competition. Perhaps that would put her at ease. Sometimes veritable hags turn his head on the street. What does he see in them? When they have sex, he sometimes wants them to watch porn and takes old DVDs out of a cabinet.

"Are these from, like … the eighties?" she asks, incredulous.

"Does it matter?" he says. "People have been having sex the same way since the dawn of time."

The films don't arouse her one bit.

"Could we find something more modern?" she suggests.

"We'd have to stream in that case," he says, "which would fill my work computer up with crap."

He tells her about Pornhub. He read somewhere that the site is visited by forty million people a day and that 90 percent of them are men. The average visit lasts eight minutes, and in those eight minutes the average visitor manages to watch 7.2 clips. Fifty percent of visitors use their cell phone while masturbating.

"Imagine that, Minnie, imagine!"

"Imagine what?" she says.

"Come on Minnie, you're not hearing me. *Eight minutes, 7.2 clips.* Can you picture it, men sitting around frantically tapping their phones while struggling to orgasm? Cell phone in one hand, cock in the other. At least with proper movies such as these, you can take your time. Get a little cozy. You can't say I'm not sensual."

She stares at the TV screen, at all the pale hairy bodies masturbating and copulating, copulating and masturbating.

"Okay," she says, "as you wish. But I don't want to see that shit. I want to feel like I'm in the modern world, so you'll have to buy another computer that we can use for this purpose alone or find a secure site."

For a moment it seems like he's considering it. But then he

shakes his head no, says maybe later, next month, if she ends up finding work as an interpreter, they can take that money and buy a computer.

Then one night, when he's had a bit too much to drink and his love for her is sort of culminating with the liquor haze, he says he loves her so much that he's going to settle for her and throw away all his porn movies. He goes into the living room, opens the cupboard, and starts tossing the eighties films on the floor. Barefoot, she keeps her distance.

"I'm not sure about this," she says. "Don't do anything rash."

"I'm doing this," he says, "as a token of my affection, and let me tell you," he adds, "this token of affection is worth more than three engagement rings."

She does in fact believe him, she says. It's tragic, but she does in fact believe him. He puts all the movies in a black bag and throws them into a container on the street. Once downstairs, he turns around, looks up at the window, and waves at her, even makes a military salute. She wonders if he has always known that when he leaves home she stands there watching him go.

"I'm going to call the council now and ask them to empty the dumpster so you won't sneak down there in the night and dig them out," she says.

He laughs. All of a sudden she feels that this subject is getting a little too much attention. She could deal with the movies. If battles can be chosen, she'd have chosen differently. And it hasn't escaped her that sometimes he'll do something apparently unexpected in order to hide something bigger. Her body slowly tenses up thinking about what it might be.

IT'S GETTING WORSE. The heat settles over Florence and the absence of a sea makes everything unbearable. In the heat, the Arno flows forth slow and brown, and as she takes her walks along the grassy banks she sees swarms of insects hovering over the water. As the temperature rises, the toxicity between them becomes more acute. She wants Ben to break the vicious cycle, to pull her out of this destructive pattern, but he doesn't succeed. Her thoughts are always with Il pulito. What is he doing now? Driving to work. The streets leading up to his warehouse are full of whores. *Puttanes, putas, putains.* An Italian industrial zone, whores from across the globe, the various degrees of misery around the world can be read by nationality. She has driven there with him and has seen it for herself. They stand in various states of undress along the road and he slows down as they drive by, he doesn't say a word but she knows not a single one escapes his gaze. She should tear herself free. All of this is vile. But it's as if he's a blazing hot stove on which she has laid her bare hands, and now they're stuck. It hurts so much to be with him but this is exactly what it's like, as if her flesh has burned onto him and when she tries to tear her hands free it only hurts more, because her hands are good and stuck and if she pulls away she has to pull so hard that *everything* comes off. Her skin, hands, arms, everything, maybe her torso too. She doesn't have that kind of strength. Better to let her hands burn. Let the flesh burn. This is the price of succumbing to charm, of letting herself be cheated, of not resisting like she should have. The women at his office. She tries not to think about them, but they keep grating, like a kind of emotional tinnitus. Sometimes its louder and sometimes quieter, but the sound is constant, ever present. Somewhere she reads that jealousy is a scorpion stinging itself, being filled with its own venom and dying. Has she already stung herself? Can she be saved?

One day Ben says he's going back to New Orleans in a few weeks. He asks if she's coming with him. She could stay at his place, he has a small pink house that he did quite a nice renovation job on after Katrina.

"What?"

She doesn't understand. He's asking if she wants to come with him to *New Orleans*? A brand-new panorama unfolds. But then she'd have to leave Il pulito, wouldn't she? She's babbling, nervously, and Ben sits there in the sun, looking at her without comment. He lets out a sudden laugh, as if she has made a fool of herself. She falls silent and looks down at the table.

"What is it?" she says.

"What are you so afraid of?" he says.

"Afraid?" she says. "Me?"

"Yes, you, Minnie," he says, laughing again.

She can't come up with a good answer. Then she sees the pharmacy sign and remembers the woman and her bodily fluids.

"I'm afraid of growing old," she says at last, "and breaking down. Of cracking."

He leans back, thinks for a moment. Then he reaches across the table, takes her hand, and says she has nothing to worry about. She has a nice little body, a body that delivers on its promises. He also says that she's a Porsche, and a Porsche might age, but it never stops being a Porsche. He goes on to say that the Porsche—she—seems to have spent a long time being driven on country roads in sixth gear. That's how the old man she's with is driving her. If that's how you want to drive your car, then you might as well get a Volvo station wagon. He, on the other hand, can rev her down and up. He knows where to put his foot, and will make sure she outdistances everyone else. If she dares. If she dares join him in New Orleans. But be aware, it's a city that takes its toll.

"What kind of toll?"

"It takes its toll," he says again. "The city has a beauty like no other but is violent in ways you can't imagine."

He says she should come along and see for herself. He also says that whatever she decides, she should leave Il pulito. He's seen her bruises, he's caught on to a thing or two. If she stays with that man, he'll kill her. Sooner or later, tomorrow or in ten years, he will kill her. At the moment of death, the realization will come to her, like a rain of glass forming a pattern before her eyes.

"And what will that pattern reveal?" she asks.

"It will reveal how godless you were when you banded together with the beast," says Ben. "Your remorse will be monumental and you will go screaming to your death. Because you will have no one to blame but yourself."

"Hell," she says.

He adds that she is a castaway, and that he's reaching out a hand from his boat. She can take it or not.

The next day she rides with him to the airport.

"I'll wait for you for three weeks," he says before heading to security. "Then I'll let you go. I'm giving you three weeks, Minnie."

ONLY ONCE BEN leaves does she realize what daily life with Il pulito has *actually* become. Even the daily life of two cheaters has its routines, a balance arises when both parties have someone else, but now Ben has gone. But he has asked her to join him. So it is more than just sex. In spite of it all, she still has Ben, Il pulito has his someone or someones that he's hooking up with at work. The proof lies in the fact that they are no longer having sex every night and somehow they've gotten used to it, accepted it. She brings this up.

"In Italy, everyone is unfaithful," she says.

He nods. "It's a kind of *sottobosco* here," he says.

They're at a bar, drinking wine and snacking on chips. The waitress is wearing tight brown leather shorts and he can't help but watch her. He simply *can't* help himself. She despises Italy, Florence in particular. All this beauty, if only it could stick to the buildings, the statues, the parks, and the views. But it creeps into the people as well, the women. They're not actually more beautiful than the women in her country, but it's the way they *administer* their beauty. They make the most of it, not to mention their men, who provide constant validation. Il pulito keeps talking about *il sottobosco*. He complains about his countrymen who so willingly dwell in this *sottobosco d'infedeltà*. The undergrowth of infidelity.

"And what about you," she says. "Do you rise like a lotus flower out of this tainted undergrowth?"

He smiles darkly, leans forward, and grabs hold of her thigh.

"Stop finding fault with me, Minnie," he says. "It's time to go home."

SIMULTANEOUS INTERPRETATION IMPROVES nothing. Long before the end of her course, she gets a job interpreting every day between nine and three, crammed inside a little booth with a buttoned-up colleague. They're supposed to trade off every fifteen minutes. She does her best, but her Italian doesn't always bear up. Her colleague hates her, she can sense it from the get-go. If a long number comes up, her colleague is expected to note it down on the piece of paper between them so that she doesn't have to hold it in her mind, but sometimes the colleague makes no notes. Her colleague just sits there, arms crossed, doing nothing. She gets mixed up, struggles to recall the numbers, and then the gist of what the speaker is saying passes her by. One day the organizer comes over to tell her that she has to shape up or they'll have to replace her. Her language neurosis intensifies. She's constantly reciting words to herself, on the way home, while doing the shopping. She'll see a car and will list its every part in three languages. Body, hood, gearbox, rims, windshield wipers. When Il pulito is talking, she's translating what he's saying into other languages. In sex, she tries to find some kind of outlet or relief. Sometimes it works. But afterward, the clouds gather again. The sickness, the neurosis, the sense that Il pulito is forever keeping her in the dark; and Ben is in New Orleans, waiting. She must do something, she must act, time is running out.

EVERY NOW AND then, since Ben's return to New Orleans, she gets the feeling that a woman has been sitting in wait outside Il pulito's door. A feeling, and because it's just a feeling for which she has no proof, she can't tell Il pulito, for risk of unleashing his by now unbridled wrath. She has noticed that ever more thin and frightful threads are being spun into the repulsive web of what their relationship has become, and sometimes she *knows* about things he has done without being able to explain how. She knows that she catches him out, and once when drunk he admits as much. Her brain is so incredibly attuned to him that it registers every little thing.

"Well yes, it's true," he says, "you *know* things, and I don't know how you do it, but it provokes the hell out of me."

She understands the mechanism. The subconscious is not subject to the laws of time and space, the subconscious can perceive things that go beyond. Jung pulled at this thread but also conceded that it was impossible to unravel the process. We know *that* it happens, he argued, but not *how*. In drunkenness Il pulito says that it's an uncanny trait of hers, sometimes she'll call with a concern right as he's about to betray her.

"Explain," she says, "when have I been right? Please, if only to allow me to preserve my sense of sanity and to understand where the line between paranoia and intuition runs through me."

He looks at her as if she were the sick one. He's the sick one really, they both know that, but he is sick *and* in control. So far they haven't said it, haven't articulated it, if he had articulated anything it would have been that she's the one who's in full control, he may be the platoon leader but she is the true five-star general. But now he says, "You'd have been a terrible commander, you'd leave only scorched earth behind you."

"I'm a very nice person," she replies, "receptive and nice, and I always bare my throat. Go ahead: Drive the knife in."

"True," he replies, "you do always bare your throat. But the moment I sink my teeth in, it's clear that your throat is ironclad."

She waves this off. It's not that simple. There is no "iron," no underlying strength that makes it possible for her to handle whatever comes her way under any circumstance. Moreover she has now degenerated, accorded a great deal of her strength to him. She has become sick. The sickness has advanced, gnawed its way deeper in, and now she is even sicker, and she is not the one steering the ship. He is sick too, it's true, but he's steering. There's a big difference. Being sick and steering the ship, or being sick and not steering the ship. In the one case, you are standing on deck, the headwind in your face; in the other, you're roving around the dark passages in the hull, not knowing where they lead, unable to spot icebergs or attacking fleets. She is in his hands, can't he see?

"*Everything is about sex except sex,*" he says in English, "*because sex is about power.* Right, Minnie? Didn't one of your writers say that? And now you're sensing that your power isn't absolute. It makes you nervous. You come from a country where women control men. But that won't fly with Mickey. When things come to a head, it's Mickey who rules Minnie, and that's that."

She's about to get hooked, get drawn in by what he's saying, but then she remembers that this isn't actually what they were discussing. They were discussing her intuition and were going to get into this matter of the woman who sometimes sits outside his door, waiting. He wants to divert her attention, but she's not about to let that happen, she's smartened up, so she sticks to the point. And the woman on the stairs is the point. She says it happens when she comes home after shopping, for example. Today she felt it as soon as she entered the stairwell, when she stepped through the front door and it slammed shut behind her and she stood there in the silence. There was a *presence.* A recently dispersed femininity in the air. It's almost always cool in the stairwell. The walls are plastered white, and the railings are made of beautifully wrought iron. She likes walking from the hot street into this space. But then she goes up the stairs, and the closer she gets to their floor, the more she feels this hypothetical presence. As if the other woman has just left, or is hiding, is standing somewhere, watching her.

Sometimes, she says to him at dinner, it's as if someone has been waiting outside our door. Has been knocking, calling *Hello, are you home, open up.*

"Waiting for what?" he says.

"You," she says. "Someone has been sitting outside, waiting for you." And she adds: "One of your many diseased whores, perhaps?"

For a moment there is silence. A dog barks in the courtyard and someone parks a moped. She knows she has crossed a line. He says he can't take it. He stands up and grabs his head, says he can't take her paranoia. He loves her, but she has to treat him with respect.

"One of your diseased whores from the street," she repeats, "because I am sure someone was sitting outside that door before I turned up."

"Where's the proof?" he says, coming toward her. "The proof for what you're alleging?"

"How am I supposed to gather any proof if you hide everything from me?" she says. "How can I gather any proof when you lie as naturally as a horse falls into a trot and you seem to be on a mission to outdo yourself bamboozling me?"

"Get over here," he says, and his gaze is black.

She stands up, turns around in a flash, and makes a run for bedroom and the bed. He catches up with her before she even reaches the threshold.

She sends Ben a picture of her beaten face. She expects sympathy, but doesn't get any. He writes:

I know there are men who get off on abused women, but I'm not of that degenerate kind. This only proves

what a lily-livered ditz you are, Minnie. What man-
ner of suffering is this, really? Is it like a warm bath
to you, a feather in your cap? You deserve that beast
of a man. I hope at least you find peace in death.

Best, Ben

At first she is disappointed. Then she thinks that settles it. She has to get out of here. She has to go to Ben, who's offering her a different life, a dignified life. She will book a ticket. Florence to London; London to New Orleans. She writes to Ben, who coolly replies sure, book the tickets, and to let him know when she's arriving so he can pick her up at the airport.

AFTER HER DIABOLICAL plan becomes a fact, Florence regains its beauty. It is still unbearably hot, but as she walks the streets it's no longer the heat she senses but the shade from the stone buildings and the trail of perfume and aftershave from the people she meets. She no longer considers ocher to be the dominant color in the city, but a pale grayish green, a calm color with hints of olive and bone-white mortar. The pedestrians all seem to be freshly showered, cooking smells waft from the tavernas, and the water in her bottle is ice-cold, giving rise to a pleasing burn in her throat as it goes down. The Arno's waters seem deeper to her, darker, cooler, and what was brown and stagnant seems to have drifted away. When she thinks of Ben and actually going to New Orleans, Il pulito shrinks in size. They stroll through the city in the evening sun.

"This is what being in Florence should feel like," she says. "Like walking around in a movie, right Mickey?"

He nods. She hums to herself. Her betrayal sits like a tangy sweetness in her chest. Whenever another woman turns his head, she smiles to herself. Just you wait, she thinks. Just you wait. They sit down at a bar in the Piazza Santo Spirito, watch the people go by. He undresses every woman with his eyes, but it doesn't bother her anymore. She thinks of Ben, what he said about her being a Porsche. Even if it was just a line, it didn't matter, because it made her happy and now she's savoring it, again and again in the warm evening air. She fantasizes about the flight.

"Have you ever been to New Orleans?" she asks Il pulito.

No, he hasn't, just Chicago, where he met an unbelievably beautiful woman.

"You don't say," she says.

Il pulito tells the tale. One of his many tales, only now it bores her. As he talks, she thinks about how one day soon she'll pack her bag while he's at work, leave a note on the table, and then be off. Whoosh, gone. Or *won't* she leave a note on the table? Will she simply disappear? She pictures him as he realizes that she and her things are gone. He'll be standing in the kitchen, incredulous. Saying: *Ma che cazzo . . . ?* Something inside him loves her beyond limit. She knows it, in spite of all the women he can't help but ogle, something of her is nailed to him. A long rusty nail driven into the depths of Il pulito, a nail he can't bring himself to pull out. For him the nail is her soul, he has fallen in love with her soul, and she has fallen in love with his flesh. A consuming imbalance. The flesh may scream more loudly, but the soul runs deeper. Flesh is commonplace, souls are harder to come by. After a few days, she'll call from New Orleans, tell him by phone how much he hurt her and that she's with another man now, he should have taken better care of her, because now she has found someone else. He should have taken better care of her, she will continue to scream. Until he gets the message. She collects herself. He'll never understand, however loud she screams. That's the problem. She can scream louder and louder, but the moment he does finally hear her, he'll kill her. He'll find a way. Such is the curse. She knows it to be so. The upward spiral of violence. He's hardly to blame, she thinks, because he doesn't have a choice. It's what the curse dictates, the one they welcomed in when they accepted this sickness and its laws. An ending has already been written for them, and it ends with her death. One night she'd asked him what he would do if he suddenly discovered that he had beaten her to death. I would shoot myself in the head, he replied. He said this without hesitation and, moreover, as if he had thought it through more than once. She looked around the room, trying to figure out where he kept his weapon, or weapons. Remembering this, she shudders a little in the hot night. And this is when he makes a fool of himself, when the waiter stops by to take their order. Il pulito says he wants a glass of "dry red wine." She manages to avert her gaze so that he can't read any condescension in her eyes, but the waiter laughs out loud and says that there are no "dry red wines." Il pulito says he meant *rough*, but the damage is done. The waiter is still laughing, does he want ice in it too? Il pulito sits there in silence, not meeting the waiter's gaze.

"Don't worry about it," she says once the chuckling waiter has gone inside to place their order.

Still he says nothing. He stands up, and she follows suit. He walks ahead of her and she can't keep pace so she starts jogging after him. One of many humiliations. One more pearl of humiliation added to the string. She'll spend the rest of the evening on the receiving end of his contempt for the waiter, he will channel it toward her, because she is also one of those many people who think they're better than him, with her high-flown idea about how working at Fiat would be a nightmare, and taking an interpreting course so she can work at conferences and speak fluently to people of all nationalities, there's something whorish about being able to do that, truly decent women don't speak that many languages, it demonstrates a certain willingness and is a turnoff, he looks down on it. And as for him, he's just some locking-system salesman. She sees the hatred in his eyes. The contempt for her worldliness, if she is to be his woman she must limit herself. She does want to. She would gladly sacrifice at least two of her languages for his undivided attention. She would give back everything she has read to live with him in a cave if it meant she'd be his one and only. He tells her to shut her trap. She thinks it's strange that the person who has such a clear upper hand in a relationship would harbor so much hatred for their underling.

She has to get out. It's the only way. And she will. The tickets are booked. She'll prepare everything. Tomorrow she will. Pack, sort out her visa online. Call Ben and have a chat, anything he wants her to bring from Florence? She has to get ready. Because one of these days this man is going to kill her. How many times has it happened now? Once is as good as never, they say, twice is two times too many. But now, twenty, thirty . . . ? Watching the sun slip behind the mountains, she realizes that she's lost count.

THAT VERY NIGHT she dreams the decisive dream, the one that will govern her every move from here on out. She finds herself with Il pulito on a moor. It is dark and the moon casts its cool shimmer across the bare earth. They are freezing cold. They are the only people around. They're deliberating. Where should they go, what should they do, how long will it be before they freeze to death? Suddenly they see two great shadows in the distance. We're going that way, Il pulito says. They approach the shadows slowly. When they arrive, they see, by the light of the moon, two stone statues. A little taller than they are, much wider, made of gray rock. Their eyes are wide open and appear to be staring straight ahead. Two stone statues, she says. Wait, Il pulito says. Something's fishy. Il pulito stands on his tiptoes and reaches for the mouth of one the statues. Although it should be impossible to lift that stony lip up, he does. He lifts it as if it were not stone but gray flesh. Inside is a mouth with red gums and the white, long teeth of a predator. They're alive, Il pulito declares in the dream. Their stillness is a pose, they're waiting. For what? she asks. He looks at her for a long time and then says: For us to

start running. What are we going to do? she whispers. I don't
know, he says. The seconds pass. The moon shines. The stone
statues wait.

The next morning at breakfast, she tells him about the
dream. Il pulito looks at her in disbelief as he chews his toast
and sips his coffee. When she's done, he nods to himself and
says, "*Cazzo Minnie, ma tu mi fai proprio paura. Chi sei?*" God-
dammit, Minnie, you're scaring me. Who *are* you?

She says what she always says: She's a completely normal
person, but this dream spoke to her, wanted to communicate
something. It was an image and it might do them good to interpret it. He shrugs.

"I don't know, I'm no interpreter of dreams, all I'm saying
is that not everybody has dreams like that. There's something
about you."

She says it doesn't matter, we are who we are, but could he
please just listen to her now.

"Let's consider something," she says.

"What?"

"Hold on. Don't be impatient. Listen to me and consider
what I'm about to say."

He holds up his hands. "I'm all ears."

"Promise to hear me out. Don't interrupt. This dream has
provided me with a theory. About us."

He looks at her with skepticism and amusement.

"Can you just listen, without any preconceptions?"

He nods and leans back in his chair. "Aye aye, captain. I'm
listening. Without any preconceptions."

"Okay, so it's like this. What if the two statues in my
dream were demons."

"*Demons?*"

"Yes, demons. And what if they've taken refuge in us and are battling something out between them? There's a demon in you, and another in me. They slipped inside us in a moment when we lost control of ourselves, when we were fighting, when things got out of hand. Or when we had sex in some ungodly way. That's when they found a way in. And the demons inside us want to hurt each other. They're using us for their own ends. Can you see? The statues in the dream were these demons. And they're simply waiting for us to start running. As long as we keep calm, they can't do anything, but if we start running, if we work ourselves up, then they'll co-opt us for their own fight. The dream means that we have to stay calm."

Il pulito grimaces. "Minnie, with all due respect . . . Now it's your turn to consider something."

"Okay."

"Could it be that you've gone crazy?"

"Crazy? No. But think about it, give it a chance. You and I are nice people, really. Or maybe not nice, but at least within the bounds of normalcy. You say you've never hit a woman before you met me and I know I've never driven a man insane before I met you. What if there's something inside of us that takes the wheel sometimes. Sometimes it wakes up and drives us. To me it seems perfectly logical that this is precisely what's going on."

Il pulito lets out a deep sigh and looks at his watch.

"It would explain so much," she says. "Don't you agree?"

"You're not well, Minnie. I'm so sorry. And I'm the one who ruined you. You were a fantastic woman, but now you're just a wreck."

"What the fuck does that have to do with anything!" she cries out. "For once, will you just listen? How we *feel* is kind of *beside the point* by now, isn't it? Can you at least think about this? Mull it over? Can you allow this possibility to exist for today so we can discuss it again tonight?"

He doesn't respond, just sits there looking at her, a crease between his eyebrows. She calms down, clears her throat, and says, "Can you trust me? Because I know that demons are the only explanation for some things There are things that lie *beyond* the light."

"What light?"

"The light. The light, Mickey, the light. Figuratively speaking, come on, make the tiniest effort."

He leans forward and looks deep into her eyes. "Minnie, it's your turn to listen to me. I'm from Puglia. You know Puglia. You've been there. You've been all over Italy and you've seen it. You've got an idea of what it can be like. Okay, good. When I was growing up, there were women who went crazy, women who had thoughts like the ones you're having. They were women without men, women who wore black every day of the week except Fridays, when they wore brown. People were afraid of them. They were unpleasant. They picked strange herbs and made potions. I fought to get out of Puglia. Puglia is a terrible place, a place where people cast the evil eye, blackmail, and blow people up. It's a truly awful—if beautiful—place. Like a beautiful, ancient whore. After having struggled so hard to get away from there, I don't want to find myself mixed up with a woman from the north who turns out to be among the worst caliber of last century's southern Italians. You know what I mean? I haven't come this far, only to go back to the place I wanted to escape. Does this make it clear to you why you can't go on like this, why I can't accept it?"

She stands up, goes to the fridge, and slugs some vodka from the bottle.

"Liquor, at eight in the morning?" he says. "Dear God, Minnie. Don't tell me the demon inside you is a drunk to boot."

He sits with his phone for a while and then gets ready for work. She sits down at the table and stares at the brick facade opposite. Before he leaves, he comes over, bends down, and mutters with his mouth to her throat, "Once upon a time there was a Minnie and a Mickey. Two lost mice crossing a great ocean, two little rodents on a raft driven by demon winds. It was so dark out there on the ocean. Minnie Mouse, said Mickey, could you give a little squeak so Mickey knows you're there . . . where are you . . . squeak squeak, Minnie . . ."

She sits perfectly still. He stands there with his mouth to her skin. As if they'd frozen to ice. How long does he stand there? How long does she sit there? For a moment she's convinced he's going to bite her, pierce her flesh, and tear out a vein with his teeth.

He goes to the hall, and soon thereafter the door slams shut behind him.

THE VIOLENCE. SOMETIMES she wishes it were more sexual, a soft sexual violence, but it's not. Arousal isn't the reason why he loses control. Not like in some stories she has heard, where the perpetrators seem to have been driven by a deep sexual urge set off in them by their victim's allure. As if the women were so irresistible that the violence could not be restrained, as if the men had to abandon their innermost core to contend with the allure of these women. This is not the case here.

She is no psychologist. True. She is no psychologist, but she has known a fair share of people, seen a thing or two, and drawn her conclusions. There's nothing secretly romantic about this violence. Somebody wrote that the face of reality is that of a castrated dog and that's a fact, the face of reality is that of a castrated dog. Reality can contain euphoria and all kinds of expanses, but when reality shows its true face, all charm is lost.

She also knows that if you've been through something truly traumatic, you don't want to talk about it. If forced to talk about it, it's always with anger, a kind of intractable resentment directed at the person who wants to listen because a person who wants to listen is also an aggressor. A lewd pleasure-seeking aggressor who wants to stare at your deepest wounds, who wants to drive their fingers into them and warm themselves in the blood and pus of your misery.

Certain victims can speak, of course, and through the repetition and dilution of experiences find relief. But unresolved trauma often lies unseen. Unresolved trauma is burdened with shame. On certain tabloid television shows, when she sees women fighting for the floor so they can recount in detail what men have done to them, she feels an aversion. Then she slowly shuts down, turns away from the world.

Il pulito's violence is pure and bitter hatred. A crude, dirty stake raised above her head.

THE FLIGHT IS drawing near. Ben is waiting for her in New Orleans. She's doing everything she can to keep things calm between them in the short time that is left. Soon she will be safe, all she has to do is keep the equilibrium for a few more days and everything will work out. Once she's on the plane, once the plane takes off, she'll be safe.

They have gone to San Gimignano for the day and are leaning against a church wall in the heat. Il pulito has turned his face to the sun.

"You're not a real Italian," she says.

"Why not?"

"An Italian would never bask in the sun like that."

"It's the northerner in me that I've adopted from you," he says.

She closes her eyes. "I might be going away for a while," she says.

"Where to?"

"I don't know. Somewhere. Somewhere where I can think and find a way back to myself."

He sighs. "You won't be able to hack it without me," he

says. "You think you can, but you can't. Just drop that idea, Minnie, it'll only put a strain on both of us if you try."

He keeps sunbathing and she keeps looking at him. His scalp is turning red. Sometimes she wakes up at night and there's a smell in the room. The first time it happened, she couldn't tell where the smell was coming from, but the second time she realized it was coming from Il pulito's head. From Il pulito's scalp. She bent over him in bed and when the smell enveloped her, she felt sick to her stomach. She knows it's the stress. She knows it's all the stress from the day that Il pulito's body is desperately trying to process at night. The smell rising from his head is some kind of by-product, a toxin that the body needs to purge but can't fit in the urine or stool, because they're already full of waste and can't cram any more in. Or . . . perhaps it's more than stress. Testosterone too. It's the stress hormones and testosterone being secreted from Il pulito's scalp at night. Can testosterone, which should be in the genitals, push its way out through the head? These aren't suitable thoughts for a sunny day in San Gimignano, she thinks, nonetheless this must be the case with Il pulito. His brain is marinating in testosterone, that's why he does what he does, that's why he has to eye up every woman he meets or go so far as to turn around and take a good look. She laughs to herself.

"If you only knew what I'm thinking about you."

"What are you thinking about me?"

"You don't want to know."

"Go on."

"No."

"Go on."

She feels something inside him start to move. The demon

stretching, waking up after a long sleep and looking around. She has to ward it off.

"I'm thinking about how afraid I am of you, Mickey."

The calm returns.

"All right, Minnie, then everything is as it should be. It's good that you're a little scared of me. You'll be more careful."

She thinks she's as dumb as a cow, but at least she's a dumb cow that has learned to stave off danger.

"Do you feel like cheering Mickey up a little?" he says.

"What would that entail?"

"You know. We'll go home, and then you'll cheer Mickey up a little."

They walk to the car. He puts his arm around her shoulder and his hand is hot in the heat, a searing piece of coal burning into her already incinerated body.

SHE LIES THERE with her fingers in the hot mud. The sickness is so pleasant, a kind of soul-corroding manicure. In the morning, after she has had her coffee, eaten a muffin, slugged some vodka from the bottle, and gone back to bed, the sickness is so pleasant, a wood-fired sauna on a cold winter night. Soon she'll leave and get well, but first she'll revel in the hot mud a bit longer. She thinks about how the demon inside her sometimes seems to sleep for long stretches at a time, and how peaceful she feels inside when it does. When the demon is sleeping, everything feels so different, as if it never existed. When they were sitting with their backs against the church in San Gimignano, for a moment everything had that sense of calm. Was it because it was a sanctuary? Or is it like during pregnancy—the baby is rocked to sleep inside you during the day, only to be awakened by the stillness when you lie down to rest at night?

Sweet it is, in any case, this sickness.

ONE DAY, WITH only a week or so to go before her flight to New Orleans, Il pulito comes home with a surprise. A bright yellow, slightly stiff envelope. He offers it to her.

"Open it," he says contentedly.

She opens it. It contains a business card for a *dottoressa*, a psychologist, by the name of Anna Chiara dei Grassi.

"Yes?" she says. "And?"

"We're going to see her," he says. "We're both going to go get our heads screwed on straight."

"What, I'm sorry . . . ?" she says.

He looks at her and if Il pulito can beam, that's exactly what he's doing. Il pulito's black eyes are beaming with joy and anticipation.

"You're going to get rid of your paranoia, stop believing in demons, and I'm going to stop hurting you all the time. First and foremost, I'm going to stop hitting you. We'll stick together. We're too broken to deal with an ending. We're so crippled by all the damage we've done to each other that if we can't get our relationship under control, we'll be forced to live with our damage in another relationship. So it's much better for us to take care of each other and heal together. Right?"

She listens wide-eyed. She says she has to go pee. She sits on the toilet and thinks about the extent of her planned betrayal. With this initiative, Il pulito is showing that he is at least sincere in his love. She is not. She's underhanded, because she's found a way out. Il pulito wants them to see a psychologist, to get a grip on themselves and start working. He's imperfect and driven by lust, yet somehow on the level. The tears come. Il pulito knocks on the door.

"Minnie?"

"Yes," she sobs, "I'm touched, that's all."

She flushes and goes into the kitchen, opens the fridge, and knocks back some vodka.

"A psychologist, huh?"

"I talked to my sister," he says, "told her everything, about how you're feeling and how I've hit . . . been acting. She said that this is the only solution. This lady is supposed to be a good psychologist."

You start by talking one-on-one, his sister had said, then together.

They go to their first appointment the very next day. He has showered, put on cologne, and is holding her hand tight. He doesn't look at a single other woman on the way. He's paying. Two sessions at seventy euros each. She's not allowed to nag him about paying her fair share. He's becoming a new man now. He's the one responsible for her sickness, her brain has misfired because she can't handle the love she has for him. He asked her to be weak and she obeyed. She trusted him and he destroyed her, but now he's going to make it right because he loves her and what he wants most of all is to get back that the high-flown woman she once was. Walking by his side, she feels more underhanded than ever. High-flown woman: Fuck off and die. She has to go into this with honesty and sincerity. Therefore she must let go of Ben and give this new thing a chance. She decides to do just that: Let go of Ben and give this new thing a chance.

He goes first, takes the first session with la dottoressa. La dottoressa's office is in her apartment, which is on the top floor of an old ocher building with turrets, not far from the Piazza della Signoria. She waits in the courtyard, where there is a laurel tree and a fountain gurgling in the shade. She sits near the tree, because laurels are sacred, and if there is a demon inside her, its power will be diminished by the sanctity of the tree. She feels the calm spreading through her body as she listens to the water. Italy, she thinks. Why live anywhere else? Each year spent somewhere other than Italy is a waste of time, a waste of life.

When Il pulito comes down, he looks so glazed his face is inscrutable.

"Your turn," is all he says. "I'll wait in the café down the street."

He's not accustomed, she thinks, to talking about his inner self, not accustomed to opening up, that explains his expression. She, on the other hand, will manage, she has talked about her inner self before, though not since this degeneration, but back when she had friends she did, and her friends would also talk about what was going on inside them and that's how they encountered each other, understood each other, helped each other. They read self-help books and supported each other.

She walks up the stairs, through a tall door made of dark wood.

"Hello? *Posso*?" she calls into the half-light of the apartment.

"*Entra, bella, entra*," la dottoressa replies.

She enters the room. La dottoressa is enormous. She is sitting on a sofa in the middle of a spacious living room and her body seems to have flowed out around her in a way that might make it impossible for her to get up at all. Behind her, through the large windows, is Florence and beyond the city, the mountains.

"Oh," she says, "how beautiful."

La dottoressa nods graciously and tells her to have a seat on the sofa.

"So tell me," she says.

She doesn't know what to say. La dottoressa smiles encouragingly and tilts her head.

"Go ahead."

But she can't, she doesn't know where to start, in the middle of it all, or at the beginning, she just knows that she has to tell the story in detail and rationally so that la dottoressa can grasp all the threads. After a while, la dottoressa seems to have grown impatient and says, "He's a lot of man, isn't he?"

"What do you mean?"

La dottoressa gives a slow shrug. "It's hard for a woman to be with a man who's so much man. It's like riding a wild bull.

You have to hold on tight, bear up against the bucking, and believe it's worth the effort."

She doesn't know what to say to that. Perhaps "There's probably enough woman in me to handle a man like him," or something succinct like "I've been through worse." Of course she hasn't, so instead she says, "I love him. We're in a rut and need help getting back on track."

La dottoressa smiles. It's a patient smile, the kind of smile a doctor gives a patient. She says he told her he has used violence against her. Is this true?

"Yes, it's true, but—"

And this is why, la dottoressa interjects, she must leave him. If he has used violence against her, she must leave him. Immediately.

"But we've come to you for help," she says, "to get well. He's not the only one who's sick, I am too."

La dottoressa sighs and shakes her head with resignation.

"He's the one who wanted to come here," she continues, "he's the one who took the initiative, he's even the one who's paying. We really want to fight for this. I mean, just try to get a man like him to see a psychologist. An ex-bodyguard from Bari. If you ask me, it's a miracle. *Se me lo chiedi a me è proprio un miracolo.*"

"I understand," says la dottoressa, "but I know it won't work. You don't seem to have any insight into how these things work. But I do, and I'm telling you: It won't work."

"How do you know?"

"Or it might work, but it will take so very much more than a few conversations."

"Lobotomizing him is out of the question, if that's what you mean."

"Exactly. And that's why it would be best if you could simply leave him."

"Leave him, and leave Florence?"

She takes in the view behind la dottoressa and feels tears welling in her eyes. All of a sudden she doesn't understand how she's supposed to leave Florence. She doesn't understand how she could have made those plans with Ben, because how can a person in full possession of their faculties leave a city like Florence and a man who may not be God's best child, but who loves you and wants to fight for you?

"Exactly," la dottoressa says. "Leave him, and leave Florence. If Italy is the sticking point, there are many other beautiful cities, Florence is not the only one."

No, but Florence is her city, their city, it's where her heart has taken root. It's these streets, this light, it's where she wants to be, where she wants to live.

"And once you've left Florence, it's crucial that that you don't answer any of his calls, don't answer any messages, *not under any circumstance*. You must steel yourself as probably never before."

"Impossible."

"Of course it's possible."

She shakes her head. "It's not possible. There's a force, something I can't control. I simply can't."

"It's really quite simple," la dottoressa says. "Put away your cell phone and sit on your hands. If you sit on your hands, you can neither answer nor write. Let it be a last resort."

A tear rolls down her cheek. She quickly wipes it away. She doesn't want la dottoressa to think she's the crying type of woman. She's more Latin than that, she can grit her teeth and suffer through it, if need be.

"He has an obsessive personality," la dottoressa continues. "He's also a narcissist. I only needed a few minutes with him to get a clear picture. Working with that kind of person is a Sisyphean task. You'll end up giving so much of yourself and getting so very little back. It's like farming in the desert. You can choose a different soil, you can sow where you can reap. Take to your heels, and leave the desert of him behind you."

She shakes her head. The more la dottoressa paints Il pulito black, the more her affection for him seems to grow.

"No, no," she says. "What would happen to him then?"

"What would happen to *him*? Don't trouble yourself with that. His personality type has to be cut off with one sure stroke. Like a snake's head. One stroke, and then you move on, no looking back. Otherwise it can get pretty dangerous. Believe me, I've seen some things."

She sits in silence. Presses her lips together. Looks at la dottoressa, and the view behind her. The sun is setting and the city is achingly beautiful in the evening light.

"He's paying for this," she says again, a little gruffly. "He's paying for my hour too. Isn't it a bit deceitful of you to advise me to leave him? Isn't his doing this an indication of how prepared he is to fight?"

La dottoressa shakes her head and leans toward her.

"You don't understand," she says. "*Ma tu non capisci proprio.* I'm talking to you woman-to-woman. I don't have to take payment for your hour if it makes you feel better, I don't care, the important thing is that you understand. What he does to you can't be changed at the drop of a hat. One fine day he'll kill you. Someday he'll crack your skull, break your neck, or strangle you. That's what I'm trying to prevent by speaking frankly."

She laughs dryly. "But I love him."

La dottoressa draws a deep sigh.

"Love," she says. "That word, so battered, so abused."

"And you say 'what he does to me,' but do you know what I do to him? You haven't asked. You haven't asked anything about what I do to provoke his anger."

La dottoressa grabs her forehead and sighs again.

"The self-belittling conviction of the abused woman. You defend him more than he defended himself when he sat here a moment ago. It's almost a bit eerie to watch."

"But what do you know?" she shouts at la dottoressa. "What do you know about him?"

"*Ma calmati*, calm down," la dottoressa says. "This, what's happening between you and me here in this room, is also normal. You two are not unique, not a special case, you are not alone in your tragedy. There are shelves upon shelves of books about people like the two of you, about the mechanisms by which you are operating right now. Abused women often take responsibility for their situation. It's an unconscious way of convincing yourself that you can do something about it. Only a person who has a responsibility can make an impact, right? And you think you can make an impact. But you can't."

She spitefully replies: sure, all that might *sound* good, and la dottoressa probably has a whole battery of good lines she can fling at people like her. But what she's saying is not true, not firmly established. Has la dottoressa herself ever been beaten? No, la dottoressa shakes her head and says she's never been hit. She has a very nice husband and they don't hit each other. Well then, she says, la dottoressa has no idea what she's talking about. The woman may have read a lot of theory and have a nice little husband that she doesn't have sex with, but she doesn't know in her flesh what it is she's talking about. In her flesh. *Nella sua carne.* That's the problem, she continues, the people who talk about this kind of abuse have rarely been abused themselves. So you have to *explain* it to them, as she is doing now to la dottoressa, and when you explain it to them, they don't understand, they just think you're ruined, indoctrinated, defending the indefensible. She tries again to explain. The fact that she's the one who provokes his anger does not *justify* anything in his reaction, but it does *explain* it.

"Do you understand?" she says, exhausted. "*Justify* is not the same as *explain.* But if I'm calm, then he's calm too."

La dottoressa clearly doesn't understand her. She sits there shaking her head.

"I don't really know what to say," la dottoressa finally says. "I just think you're incredibly foolish."

"And that's what you, in your professional opinion, have to say to me?"

"Yes. If the truth be told, that's all I have to say. You're *incredibly* foolish. *Incredibilmente scema.*"

La dottoressa emphasizes every syllable. Anger rising, she looks la dottoressa in the eye and says what does an obese woman know about passion, it's impossible to be passionate if you look like a wandering fatberg. She can just picture that nice little husband climbing the fatberg, but what next? That's her question. What does he do next?

"There's no need to be disrespectful," la dottoressa says coldly.

In fact there is. La dottoressa has not had sex for ages, it's in the air, because people who don't have sex give off a particular scent of stagnant bodily fluids, and she can smell it. La dottoressa's husband is like a Christmas bauble that la dottoressa has to have in her life in order to feel like she is complying with the norms of this damned bigoted hellhole of a Catholic society.

La dottoressa wets her lips with her tongue.

"You're not well," she says. "A moment ago you said Italy was fantastic and that you couldn't leave it, that it's the country you love as well, not the man alone, and now you're saying the country is a hellhole. You're not well. You need help."

"I suppose I'm what one might call *ambivalent*."

"I'm saying you're not well. You need to get help."

"But you're not helping me! You can't, you won't, you just want to put down me and the man I love! Your books tell you how things stand, and those books are written by other deluded dottoressas who haven't lived the problem in their flesh either. *In their flesh*. Do you understand?"

She gets up, says she's leaving, this was money down the drain.

La dottoressa says, "One last thing."

"What?" she says.

"Nothing, and I mean nothing, can get hold of a person who isn't swimming with their barbs out."

"What do you mean?"

"Exactly what I said. That if he gets hold of you, it's because you're swimming with your barbs out. He gets hold of you because you're making yourself available."

She doesn't respond. She just walks out. But once through the hallway and nearing the top of the stairs, she slows down. She stops mid-step and turns around. She smooths her hair, adjusts her dress, and goes back into la dottoressa, sits down on the sofa, and crosses one leg over the other.

"Um," she says, "there was one more thing."

"Yes?" la dottoressa says flatly.

"Well, the thing is, I wonder if you think it might be possible that we have been possessed by two demons?"

La dottoressa stares at her. She thinks she sees a hint of a sneer in la dottoressa's eyes, a sneer that la dottoressa manages to curb before it is revealed. She continues.

"I imagine that there are two demons fighting a battle, and the two demons are using us as their bodies. Their lairs. Devil's lairs. Have you ever heard of such a thing, a devil's lair?"

La dottoressa wets her lips again.

"No," she says, shaking her head, "I most certainly have not."

"I understand that you're upset because I just insulted you, and perhaps you no longer feel that I deserve an answer or help, but I would still be very grateful if you could respond to my question as honestly as possible."

La dottoressa clears her throat and seems to be fumbling for words.

"You're saying that you believe in demons," she says at last.

"Believe?" she says. "No, I don't believe. I *know* they exist. I've been through things in my childhood that leave me no doubt. For years I lived only a few miles from a great demon. It would be impossible not to believe in them."

La dottoressa stares at her. "I understand," she says eventually, "but no, this is not the case, it is not the case that you have been possessed by two demons. What you are demonstrating is a psychological defense mechanism called dissociation. Your brain is doing this because it can't fit all the pieces together, it doesn't understand the fact that you're staying with this man, and to avoid confronting reality it splits you into different figures. So far there is only you and the demon, but more may appear. It could also be that you have been subjected to sexual violence and that the dissociation stems from post-traumatic stress."

"I see," she replies dryly, "unbelievable. Well, I tried."

"Tried what?"

"To open up and communicate. But you have too many preconceived notions to see the whole picture."

La dottoressa sighs.

"By the way, this only proves what I've been feeling throughout this conversation."

"Really?" la dottoressa says, worn out. "And what's that?"

"That you're a lousy psychologist."

"A lousy psychologist?"

"Yes. Because a good psychologist can speak the patient's language. If you were a real psychologist, like Jung, for example, then you would have said that yes, there is a demon, and then you would have helped me to get rid of it. Whether or not there is a demon, whether or not *you* believe it. You would have inhabited my perception of reality and helped me influence it from within. But that's not what you're doing. You're speaking to me as if I were not myself, you're speaking to me as if I were a colleague with whom you could discuss the case of me."

La dottoressa looks at her in the silence. Finally, with great effort, she turns herself around, rummages among the books on the shelf behind her, picks one up, and leafs through it. Then she looks up and says, "Is this what you mean?" She reads aloud from the book: "*What are we supposed to say to our patient with the imaginary cancerous tumor? I would say: Yes, you are de facto suffering from something cancerous. You are in fact harboring an irreconcilable evil, but it will not kill your body, because it is imaginary. However, in time it will kill your soul. It has already corrupted and poisoned your human relationships and your ability to feel joy. It will continue to spread until it has devoured your entire psychological existence, so that at last you are no longer human but only a horrid, consuming tumor.*"

"Exactly," she nods eagerly and victoriously. "That's what I meant. That's how Jung went about it, and that's why he was infinitely more successful than you are."

"Listen carefully," la dottoressa says, setting the book aside. "If we'd had the time, we could definitely have played Jung and the cancerous tumor. We could have sat here analyzing what you think is your demon, we could have picked it up and held it to the light, yes, contemplated its bottomless evil and black heart. I could have entered your brain through the back door and worked my way to some kind of therapeutic approach to your problems. But the thing is, we don't have time. We're not Jung and the tumor in a big house in Switzerland overlooking a lake with a clock ticking calmly in the background. We're somewhere else entirely. You're sitting on the tracks and a train is not only approaching, it has already appeared behind you, it's coming for you, full steam ahead, and you must—*must*—hurl yourself out of the way! That's where we are. Forget Jung, forget the tumor. This is about life and death in the here and now, and time is about to run out."

She feels deflated. Misunderstood, deflated, rebuked. She wants to tell la dottoressa that she's a patronizing *Besserwisser*, but instead she says, "You're *sweating*."

La dottoressa smiles sadly. "Am I? Oh, yes. Well, it's no picnic talking to you."

"Isn't that what you're trained to do? To talk to people like me?"

"Indeed. But I do think our time is up. Seventy euros only go so far."

"I want his money back. I don't want him to have paid seventy euros without me getting any help."

"It would have taken much longer to help you," says la dottoressa with a short, hollow laugh.

"Give me the money."

"Certainly, take it easy, I'll give you your money, but understand one thing: There is no demon. There are only people. Confused, stressed, and thoughtless people, people who seek relief through their lust, their violence, their egoism, and their sickness. That's all there is. No demon, no devil's lair, just the two of you, the two of you acting like two monsters, nothing more. People, only people!"

La dottoressa has tears in her eyes. Again with great difficulty, she turns around in her chair and opens a box on the table and takes out three crumpled banknotes.

"Here," she says, tossing the notes at her. "Here's the sweaty money your boorish man gave me. Now go, and leave me in peace."

She bends down and picks up the notes from the floor. Then she leaves la dottoressa and the magnificent view of Florence and starts walking through the hall. As she is about to leave the apartment, she turns around and sees la dottoressa reading the book about Jung and the cancerous tumor. She is sitting perfectly still, as if frozen to ice in this heat.

She walks down the stairs, past the gurgling fountain with the laurel tree, and onward to Il pulito in the café. Before she enters, she looks through the window to see if he's talking to anyone. He isn't. He is sitting with his phone, the very picture of innocence.

On the way home, she wonders what the psychologist said to him. He says she told him that he's an egotist.

"Did she say narcissist?"

Il pulito thinks. "No, I think it was egotist. Though it could have been both. Egotist and narcissist."

"And what do you think about that?" she says.

"She's absolutely right," he says.

"Doesn't that feel like an insult?"

"No," he says. "I am. But even egotists have a right to be loved, don't they? How else can we become better people unless somebody loves us?"

She smiles. "Yes," she says. "Exactly. How can you become better a person unless somebody loves you?"

They walk in silence. She takes his hand. It's a little sweaty, but big, safe, and warm.

"And you," he says. "What did she say to you? Next stop psych ward, right?"

She shrugs. "Nothing much, really. Just psychobabble, you know. *Blah, blah, blah, you're like this and like that, and your childhood this and your childhood that,* and so on."

He nods. "Yes," he says. "That's the kind of thing they say."

"Yes," she says. "They've got their repertoire."

"Do you want to go back?" he asks.

She shakes her head. "No," she says. "I appreciate you for taking the initiative, but I don't think psychologists are for me."

He slides his arm around her waist and pulls her close.

"Isn't that the truth," he says. "It might work on normal people, but not on people like us."

"Exactly. Maybe on normal people, but not on people like us."

She looks at him, and for a brief moment the two of them are smiling.

THE FOLLOWING EVENING, she is gripped by the realization that she must see her plan through after all and go to Ben. The visit to the psychologist provided a kind of respite from her misery, but she can't back out now. She realizes that she has lost all steadfastness, she is being tossed this way and that, her inner compass is broken and the needle is spinning in desperate search of true north. But at least she doesn't have to explain her inner grappling to anyone because she is all alone. That's the beauty of solitude, she thinks victoriously. You don't have to explain anything. The recruiting agent has informed her that they've found another interpreter, so she isn't needed anymore. She sits in the apartment. Her cell phone lies silent on the table. She feels that she has somehow drawn upon herself another curse, that she has been locked out of Eden once and for all, and that she is now not only beyond sense but also beyond salvation. She is aboard a great ship on churning seas, sailing on her own, and so must stand for every decision about the progression of the voyage. She must not slip up because certain slips can only happen once, and deep down she does not in fact want to die.

But that very evening, there is an escalation. She can't restrain herself. She screams that she hates every single one of his whores. She provokes him like never before. But she also notices something that happens right before the situation gets out of hand. She becomes aware that there is a moment, a brief moment before the fear and panic arrive, when she takes pleasure in losing control. Do not gaze into the abyss, Nietzsche wrote, because in the end the abyss also gazes into you. This is what's happening. The abyss has sensed her gaze and slowly turned its gaze upon her. It is staring into her and robbing her of all power. Total apocalypse, the blows ache, sting, and burn. But in the midst of the pain and confusion there appears a sudden shimmer, a shining spasm of sickness that permeates her whole being.

WHEN SHE WAS a child, her mother used to say that she had a small, but not insignificant, chip of ice in her heart. It was wedged, securely, between the valves and would probably stay there until she died. The chip of ice, according to her mother, had a protective effect, as it kept a part of her emotional life numbed.

"May it never thaw," her mother would say to other adults, "because if it does my daughter will suffer from excessive sensitivity, the kind of sensitivity that no human being can bear in the long run."

That's what her mother said to the other adults if anyone had any opinions about her.

But to her mother, the chip of ice was not a mere assertion, it was also a hope, a wish. After that ten-year-old girl was tortured, murdered, dismembered, and found in a garbage bag, it was as if all the mothers in the village lost their minds. Her mother's gaze could turn so despairing, so wild, so beside itself at the slightest infraction on her part. Staying out a smidgen past curfew, not calling home if she visited a friend after school, taking a walk in the woods after dark. Her mother's anxiety was draining, suffocating, an umbilical cord wound round and round her neck and then tightened like a choke chain at the slightest hint of the unexpected. The village's every scar. The scars etched on her heart. Her mother's hope in the chip of ice. May my daughter forever hold that chip of ice in her heart, may it never thaw, may it allow her to never fully experience the horror.

DURING THESE LAST days in Florence, while making coffee in the morning, she thinks of herself as dead. And in doing so she does not picture a heaven, for she knows that anything like it is out of the question for her. At best, she will go nowhere at all, and at worst, she will end up in hell. It happens that she wakes up at night and thinks about this hell. Sometimes she even descends into hell. She knows she shouldn't, but she can't help it, because hell is like the sickness, maybe the sickness and hell are even one and the same. They cannot be resisted. The dark maw of hell is too inviting, the smells wafting up from it are not as unpleasant as they say. You feel the hotness on the soles of your feet. That's when her blood, her deep-frozen Scandinavian blood, thaws. Sometimes she hears their voices down below. His and hers. It happens that she laughs, not without tears in her eyes, for it is lovely to hear their voices, friendly and engaged, in conversation. She remembers her frostbitten inner garden, the sunbeams that thawed the earth. But one day she won't remember, and neither will he. One day they will both be gone, and in all likelihood there will be no one who thinks of them. Perhaps he will be the last thing she sees before she dies. How awful that would be, but not entirely unlikely. One of his fake smiles, the varnish on every betrayal. As for him, she imagines that she will be last thing he'll see before he dies. She's standing over him, and she does not look happy.

SO THE DECISION is finally made: She's leaving the day after tomorrow. The heat is like a paralyzing haze in the attic apartment, but the decision fulfills her now, makes her almost euphoric, and Il pulito is incapable of seeing that her euphoria stems from anything other than him. He has never doubted his status as the natural source of *all* her joy, and this is why he in turn can find such joy with her. Men love it when you're happy, she thinks, it's as if they're being absolved of some sort of original sin.

"I love it when you're happy like this," he does in fact say, with tears in his eyes. "You are the love of my life, and I am so sorry for the hurt I've caused you. I will never hit you again, Minnie, please cover the bruises up so I don't have to look at them."

He embraces her and suggests they go out for lunch. She feels a little ashamed, after all she is in the process of leaving him for someone else—but she has to think according to the simple equation of violence now, that once you've hit someone you deserve all manner of violation against you for all time. You are banished from decency. He has been banished, and if she is to heed la dottoressa's advice (her surely and in spite of everything very wise advice), then she need not feel guilty, she can do what she likes to him, for he is a simple perpetrator of violence who deserves to be given hell.

Her soul feels a little tender, tender for him, because as they're eating she is once again plotting each step of her escape. While he eats and talks—happily, it should be said—while he eats and talks happily, topping up her wine and playing footsie under the table, pressing his foot between her legs, she's thinking of how to go about leaving him. Upon the arrival of lemon sorbet, she is once more imagining the look on his face when he comes home from work and realizes that she's gone. The moment his eyes meet the note on the table. He'll be left standing there.

She will prepare everything as soon as he has gone off to work. Write to Ben. Iron, pack. She's already made a list of everything she mustn't forget. Finally, she'll place a note on the table saying she's gone away, the reason being that she needs time to think. When they return home after lunch, he wants to have sex. He pulls her toward the bed but she breaks free and takes a seat on the couch. That's her limit. She can't have sex with him however often now that she's decided to leave him for Ben. She's not perfect, but she wants to be a one-man woman and does what she can to be just that. She says she has an itch down there, and it might be a yeast infection. He accepts this, says he *respects* her refusal. She sees that he is doing his best to be a good man. She sees the effort he's making, because he wants to forget everything that once was, he wants her to be happy and he wants to be a good man for his happy woman. That's what he wants for them now. One of his friends calls and she hears him say that she's keeping him celibate. She can hear that he's joking around, but she also hears the darkness behind this quip. In the evening, he creeps close and asks if he can hold her. She pretends to be asleep, but lets him pull her close. She can feel his hard-on, but pretends not to. After a while it goes away and she can tell by his breathing that he's asleep. Images move through her mind: her wetting the bed, the bat flying under the wooden roof, them driving past the whores in the industrial zone, the door slamming behind him when he leaves home, la dottoressa crying over her stupidity. She can feel his strength in her flesh, the consequences of his strength in her flesh, the consequences of his strength and her stupidity in her own flesh.

On the other hand. As long as he does not turn this strength *against* her, it's as if it is at her disposal as well, which has its own distinct allure. He is a dangerous animal, but she can master him. Sometimes anyway, sometimes she succeeds at this: at *manipulating* him. If he found out, he'd kill her that instant. If he knew what she was planning with Ben, he'd sit up wide-awake in bed, raise his fist, and beat her until her head split open. *Finche non si rompe la testa, hasta que la cabeza se parta*, until the skull cracks. Nothing makes him more furious than being manipulated. She has tried to explain that a person resorts to manipulation when they have no power, that's when manipulation comes into play, there is no malice in it really. *Can't bullshit a . . .* comes the laconic reply.

SO SHE LEAVES the apartment. She didn't think it was possible, but it is. Once it is done, it's like going to the supermarket or the hairdresser, you put one foot in front of the other, cross the threshold, and off you go. She takes her suitcase, locks the door, and jogs down the stairs to the taxi waiting on the street. She is freshly showered, her hair is wet, and her body is in a fresh state of tension, as if she were about to do something illegal, as if she were embarking on a secret mission, smuggling drugs or spying. But in fact she's just running away from the man who beats her. That's the perspective she has to adopt, or else she'll never follow through. She tells herself: I'm only running away, and I'm doing it to save myself. But she gleans the duplicity in these words, as if worms of untruth were crawling around in them. Crawling around, ingesting, poisoning, hollowing out. But isn't there truth in this? Hasn't the man she's now running away from almost killed her more than once? Isn't this *the only* truth that has the power to save her? Yes! It is. If she wants to live, she must think of herself as good and Il pulito as evil. She is good and Il pulito is evil, she is good and Il pulito is evil. From here on out, that statement must not, under any circumstance, be tampered with.

She hums to herself. The door leading to Il pulito's stairway slams shut behind her. She is standing on the street. The light is different today, friendlier somehow. Even the buildings around her, with their balconies and gardens, look friendlier, as if the residents behind the gates welcomed her departure.

As the plane takes off from the airport in Florence, she looks out over the landscape. The city appears to be in a basin, like the bottom of a cauldron. All around, the rolling landscape, small villages dotting the hills. In that cauldron she'd lived her life, in that basin and on those slopes they would drive around. Il pulito behind the wheel and she beside him, sunroof open and music on. She realizes that she might be getting a little healthier already, even though she has merely boarded a plane, for distant is the joy of testosterone-laden sweat, cool church walls, and ocher-tinged mystery. Now she rather thinks there is something cruel about that beauty, something frosty and overwrought. One cannot trust beauty that carries with it the possibility of such filth, such degradation. The airplane rises through the cloud cover and suddenly everything becomes clear, illuminated, and ice-cold.

She is awake all the way to London but after the plane departs from Gatwick she takes her sleeping pill. She doesn't like transatlantic flights. The feeling of flying over an ocean of black water and chasmic depths, flying while considering the possibility that she might be harboring a demon, is more than she can handle right now. She doesn't wake up until the plane is above Louisiana. By now Il pulito has come home. He's read the note and knows she's gone. He's called and called, but the cell phone in her bag is shut off and she's not even considering switching it on after she gets off the plane. He has called his friends and they have discussed what might have happened. In all likelihood, someone has picked him up and taken him out for beers. Or he's met up with a lover, or—if he's really desperate—driven out to the industrial zone. Perhaps his potency has taken a hit. A cold fist grabs hold of him when he thinks about her being gone. The loss is too great, even for someone with a libido as solid and all-encompassing as his.

Her escape is going well, she thinks calmly, her escape is exceeding expectations.

But as the body of the airplane approaches New Orleans, she is filled with an irrational, paralyzing fear. What is she up to, really? She sees the miles-wide swamp, its water meeting the sea along the frayed coastline, she sees fresh water flowing into salt water and the salt flowing into the fresh, forming a brackish no-man's-land that seems to shine, stagnant and insalubrious. She imagines the city they are flying toward and its inhabitants. By turns people and reptiles, and all the filth that the river's outflow must contain. She imagines the swamp having found its way into the sewage system and how the subterranean is teeming with tiny alligators, frogs, snakes. She imagines them crowding under the streets, and how they too, at some unlikely moment, might break through the earth's surface and spill into the houses. She sees the Mississippi River flowing through the city, like a winding fairway for malady and pestilence. Giant boats that look like steam-powered ocean liners are on the river. In the airplane, a man sitting nearby is telling another man that those vessels sound their horns all night long, and sooner or later the drawn-out wailing that pierces the city in the small hours makes New Orleanians lose their minds. She thinks of Florence. The olive-hued facades, the evening sun, the hustle and bustle, the heat, the people. She thinks that living here will be no mean feat.

"And it's this phenomenon that makes the city so unbelievably violent," the man continues, "because New Orleans is one of the most violent cities in the entire United States. People go crazy, they can't hack it, they go out and kill, because that's how humans function when they get stressed, they go out and fight and kill. They go on the defensive, and when there's nothing to defend themselves against, they attack."

The man falls silent. She wants to get off this plane. What has she gotten herself into? How well does she know Ben, really? She has up and left Il pulito, did he really deserve that? Do people who, despite their monumental and undeniable flaws, have loved you so much that they've been driven to the brink of madness deserve to be left without a word, without a reasonable explanation? She doesn't want to be like this. She wants to be good, generous, and reassuring, but what is a good, generous, and reassuring person supposed to do when she finds herself in a situation like this? How did it come to this? Maybe certain people don't end up in certain situations. It's as if some people are Teflon-coated, anything negative rolls right off, nothing can get their hooks in them. They stand *above*. They stand above the aggression, the hysteria, and the lack of self-control. Ben is like that. She'd probably always thought that she was like that too: a person who manages to keep things in check, who may suffer on the inside but who makes sure to keep her distance so as not to outwardly snap. Until she met Il pulito. Then everything went downhill and now she has run out of self-confidence. There is no longer any doubt. This is a new element in her life. Her confidence has been such that she has never had to dwell on it. She never had any doubt about how to comport herself in various situations, she has never had to twist or turn things around, her days have not been weighed down by dilemmas. If your days are weighed down by dilemmas, it's because you're on the wrong path. The right path is simple. The right path brings peace of mind.

Instead, she's sitting inside this monumental carapace slowly descending on an alien city. There are points of no return, and this is one of them.

She collects her luggage and heads for the arrivals hall. Ben is standing there.

"Hello," he says.

He doesn't look as happy as she would have hoped. He seems a little low in spirits, guarded. The disappointment makes her unable to hold out any longer, so when they're in the car and Ben isn't engaging in conversation, she turns on her cell phone. Sixty-two missed calls and fifty-six messages. Turning on her phone was a mistake, now Il pulito can see that she has received his messages, making the absence of a reply from her especially arrogant. Not having seen them is one thing, it's another if she has. His heart on a tray, outstretched to her. He too has his pride. He too will be hurt *even more deeply than he already has been* if she doesn't answer. But she is far away and he can't reach her here. He can feel hurt all he wants; she is out of reach. She turns the phone back off and stuffs it in her suitcase.

They drive away from the airport and Ben is still indifferent, verging on cold. She pictures Il pulito taking care of business at work, but he's torn up inside. By anger, by sadness. His wounded manhood cannot find peace, for the wound is too wide, deep, and dirty. But now it's tearing at her too. What she's doing is not right. She's a coward. La dottoressa would have applauded her, but deep down she knows she's betraying him for the world. What does the world know about them, what does the world know about what they've shared? What does the world know about the nights they spent sleeping next to each other, when they held each other, when their breathing took on the same rhythm, when in slumber they united? Suddenly she pictures his toes. His slanting sea-grass toes, pointing this way and that on one foot and the other. She is filled with a tenderness so potent it takes her breath away. She must be crazy. She has accepted an informal invitation, to say the least, an invitation that was also half-hearted, and if she had been a little less eager to get away she would have sensed this, that the invitation was half-hearted. Certain men make such invitations, and they do so to spare a woman the hurt, but they hope that the woman is perceptive enough to decline. She wasn't. It says something about her, and it's nothing good. A man like Ben, a friendly man who for a moment wished her well. She and Ben have had a few encounters, nothing more, and just because you think you know a person's flesh doesn't mean you know anything else about them. He saw her bruises and was moved to take pity on her, perhaps he thinks she is some broken victim that in a moment of weakness he wished he could mend.

They go to his place, a bright pink house in a cluster of colorful houses. She likes the neighborhood, she likes the city. Through the window she watches a neighbor woman from the house diagonally opposite hang long green necklaces in a tree. Then they hang there, slowly swaying back and forth in the hot Caribbean wind.

DURING HER FIRST few days at Ben's, she barely goes out. She feels a reluctance, she doesn't want to leave the house. She stands there, peering out the living-room window. It's all so different. The people, the homes. Some roofs have stayed broken ever since Katrina. Most of the buildings have makeshift tin roofs. It's as if relocating from one continent to another has activated her social anxiety. But she should make an effort to live, to be a little normal. She's afraid that if she goes out something will come to a head, she won't manage to blend in, she won't understand the codes of this new place, and Ben, as a consequence of her inability, will distance himself from her even more.

Finally she pulls herself together and leaves the house. She asks Ben if he wants to join her, but he absently shakes his head. She takes a stroll. A long street with many houses similar to Ben's. They all have small front porches. She comes to a place with two bridges spanning the area. A clutch of men are standing there. They look at her and they don't look happy. She tries to go by unnoticed, but can't resist glancing over her shoulder once she has walked past. That's when she sees that they're coming her way. The men in a row, eyes fixed on her. She stops, meets their gaze. They look at her coldly and she wants to believe in the good of everyone, to inhabit the conviction that something about her blends in here, something universally human, but there is no mistaking the threat in their eyes. She's not from here, she doesn't fit in, she's a tourist, you can tell from a mile off. She turns and speeds her steps. The men do the same, following her, faster. She starts running. They start running. She hears them laughing, one shouts out in Mexican Spanish. She feels the panic rise in her chest and runs for all she's worth. She hears them laughing again behind her and out of the corner of her eye she sees them closing in. She senses that they'd have no problem catching up with her but they don't, it's as if they want to test her endurance. They're behind her, pushing on, but not catching up. Eventually she sees the back of Ben's pink house and so she cuts through the neighbor's yard and hurls herself through Ben's back door. She lies on the floor, gasping. Then she staggers into the living room and sees Ben sitting on the couch watching TV, calmly with the remote control in one hand and a beer in the other.

"I was being chased," she says. "A gang of men were chasing me."

Ben nods. "You stick out here, and New Orleans isn't like other cities."

She goes to the window and looks outside. The men are nowhere to be seen.

"Don't you care?" she says.

"About what?"

"About me."

"Sure, but . . ." He leaves it hanging.

She faces him and gets to the point: "Be straight with me, Ben, is my being here bothering you?"

He sits there for a moment before he responds shame-faced, his voice low: "Am I bothered? No. But I don't desire you anymore."

"Why?" she says with disappointment. "What have I done wrong?"

"I don't know," he says. "I really don't."

"I've come all the way from Florence, Ben. Do you under-stand? All the way from *Florence*."

He nods guiltily. "You can't control desire."

"No, but maybe you can . . . try anyway. Let's give it a try. You might change your mind."

He shakes his head. "I think it's because I'm back in my context. Maybe ours could only work there, in Florence. Here I'm someone else and you belong elsewhere."

"*What?*" she says. "Do you realize what you're saying?"

He shrugs.

"Don't you remember?" she says. "Us lying on a blanket in the park, drinking white wine and eating medlars?"

He shakes his head. No, that particular memory fails him.

"All of it was romantic, even though the medlars were sour, the wine was lukewarm, and the tourists were like a slug-gish mass moving through the park . . . in spite of all that it was romantic because you and I were lying there, enjoying each other, you desired me and even said I was like a . . ."

But he doesn't seem to remember any of it, and instead of indulging in nostalgia, he turns off the TV, gets up, and walks out. She is left sitting on the couch. She spends a while trying to ignore her feelings. But then she runs out of the energy it takes to resist and this is when her longing for Il pulito takes hold of her heart like an iron claw.

THE NEXT DAY she wakes up alone in Ben's bed. In her half slumber she remembers: She's in New Orleans, with a man who doesn't really want her to be there. They haven't made love since she arrived and it's like living with a stranger. She's not used to being with a man who won't touch her. If Ben had put his hands on her, everything would have worked out. She knows it. If the physical is in working order, it loosens every knot. Moreover she needs to be with him to get Il pulito out of her system, it's like running a cleanup program on the computer, anything that's sitting there clogging things has to go. But Ben feels *aversion*. That's what she has to deal with now. Ben is averse to her, and she's living in his house. Yet another variable to take into consideration in an ocean of other variables that all seem to speak to her disadvantage. But she shouldn't let it get her down. As Il pulito would say: You wanted the bike, so pedal. *Volevi la bicicletta, adesso pedala.* She has come all this way and now she has to make an effort. Nothing in this life is free. But to make an effort she must have a goal. What's the goal? The goal is having a good relationship with Ben and for the people around to know that they

are together and to respect her as a part of Ben's life. Then she
can live with Ben in this little pink house, they can establish
a little life together, an everyday life, a routine as two healthy,
sensible, demon-free people.

She gets up. The dishes from a dinner they had a couple
of nights ago are still on the kitchen counter. Chicken with
orange and peanuts, several glasses of wine and neat liquor
to boot, which has begun to evaporate in the heat and is now
thick in the air. She tells herself that the dishes will have to
be priority one, because otherwise tiny critters might crawl
out of the drains. She washes the dishes and from the faucet
comes no more than a trickle that seems it might at any moment slow to a drip and then run out. It's the same when she
takes a shower shortly thereafter—the water pressure is so
low that she can barely rinse the shampoo from her hair, and
suddenly, before she's done, the water does run out. She feels
so pitiful standing in the shower, so pitiful and pathetic,
naked and covered in suds, without enough water to rinse
herself clean. She sees the bruises under the lather, glow-
ing black against the foam, the edges have turned green, lu-
minous mold-green rims around the black, swamp-colored
edges around what is broken inside her. She wants to slam the
showerhead into the wall and scream. Give her desperation
an outlet. She feels so fucking *stupid*. And she is not stupid.
She's on the wrong track, but she's not stupid. Or is she? She
doesn't know anymore. La dottoressa went so far as to call her
idiotic, and that's a strong word coming from an expert. And
everything here is so alien. The city is alien, the air is alien.
The proximity to the ocean is frightening because there are
no beaches, no properly defined shoreline, just swamp. The

river is frightening too, as are the necklaces whose swaying in the neighbor's tree seems ominous. As if the beads were eyes surveilling her. She misses Italy. The safe streets, the comfort. The water pressure, the absence of critters and stagnant air. But she has to be strong now. Nothing is easy, life is not easy, neither for her nor anyone else. She has to keep it positive and the only positive thing right now is that she has managed to resist the temptation to pick up the phone. She hasn't switched the cell phone back on and she hasn't read Il pulito's messages and because she hasn't the demon hasn't received any nourishment and so it can't wreak havoc. The demon has been as calm as can be since she left Florence. Perhaps it was forced out of her the second she left Il pulito's apartment for good. Maybe that's where it resided, maybe it was rooted to that spot. Genius loci, the kind of thing she has read about in books with court records from the seventeenth century, spirits that grew out of specific concrete places. Or maybe the demon is as confused as she is, trying to take in the newness of this city, find some sort of foothold before springing to life. Not feeding it is of the utmost importance. It will starve to death if she doesn't give it anything. No messages from Il pulito, no calls, just compact silence, that's good, right, isn't that a step forward? Yes, it's good. It's all good. *Tutto andrà bene, todo irá bien.* As long as she can stay here a while, establish her habits, *hábitos, abitudini,* get to know Ben better. Then even what is alien now will slowly but surely become a new home.

That's when she comes up with her crazy idea. It's a little after ten in the morning and she's standing in the shower, hair still full of suds and still without water, and it hits her like a bolt from the blue. In retrospect, she will think that the demon must have been of the opinion that she was feeling a little too safe in the saddle, a little too sure of her own mind, and so it sent her this idea right then. But there, in the moment, it seems marvelous, brilliant, yes, outstanding! She should invite Ben's friends over. If Muhammad won't go to the mountain . . . And since Ben hasn't taken the initiative himself (which he could have, but she's not about to stew on it), she will. So she decides to kill three birds with one stone: She'll get to know Ben and his environs better, she'll keep busy, and she'll make friends in the city, friends who can help give her a sense that, yes, she can feel at home here. The cell phone will have to stay in her bag, receiving all of Il pulito's messages. She will resist. She will see it all through, will not sneak a look at what he's writing, how many messages he's sending, how bad he's feeling without her, she will not partake in his pain and take solace in it, she will not feel the warmth spread through her chest when she sees that he's suffering as well, she will nourish herself with power from a different spring, a healthy power, the power to continue what she has now begun. The Great Change. The Final and Irrevocable Repudiation.

She plucks up her courage. Rinses out the shampoo with the despairingly weak stream of water. She has to think about what to serve and she'll need to clean the house, maybe go downtown and buy something, a nice piece of fabric perhaps, something that shows who she is and hints at how she will enrich Ben's life. Silly thoughts, she knows, but still. Cook something, something from her home country or something Italian. Friends are important, one of the problems with Il pulito was that they had no mutual friends, it was just the two of them, the two of them building their dreadful existence in a vacuum. Friends see, notice, can question something that looks like it's about to take a wrong turn. Friends. Airbags to buffer the demons. They will have friends, she and Ben will have lots of friends.

She leaves her phone behind, puts it under the mattress and goes downtown. The whole way there, it seems like such a *splendid* idea. She walks around buying food that she'll arrange as an antipasto. Ricotta with vinegar cream, she finds Spanish white wines and buffalo mozzarella flown in from Galicia and Naples respectively. On the way back to the bus stop, she passes a bookshop. She goes in for a browse. On a shelf not far from the entrance there is a book on display. Why does she even *see* it? Why does she see *that book*? Why, of all the thousands of books in there, does her gaze fall upon that particular book? She thinks, with a flicker of annoyance, that this book doesn't interest her now that she is no longer in the Situation. But it is as if the book has a magnetic charge, she is drawn to it, she wants to read descriptions of battered women and think that's how she used to be when she was the unfortunate person who was with Il pulito, then she was hectored and idiotic but look at her now, at how she broke free. She walks up to the book. It's written by a journalist called Rachel Louise Snyder and its title is *No Visible Bruises*. She turns to a page at random and her eyes fall on a line that suggests the level of danger rises during a specific timeline, which typically begins when the victim considers leaving the relationship and seeking help. It also says that *the danger* is highest during the first month, it decreases slightly after six months, and the victim is as good as out of danger a year after breaking up with and cutting off contact with the perpetrator. The perpetrator. She feels a kind of triumphant superiority when she reads that word. Il pulito, or if you please: the Perpetrator. The choice of words truly does bolster her. He's not a real person, he's *the Perpetrator*. Leaving *the Perpetrator* was one of the best things she's ever done in her life. Now all she has to do is stay the course. Not pick up the phone she left at Ben's house, and if she picks it up later today, she will not open the messaging app, and if she opens the messaging app to write to Ben, she will not tap Il pulito's name. She knows that he knows how to ensnare her, he can write things that will make her want to respond right away, no matter how she has fortified herself. She may have a low opinion of his character, but she is aware that he is a splendid manipulator and that he always plays on her inner keys like the most dexterous of soulful concert pianists. Il pulito can always find the melody to which her interior will respond. Il pulito may lack empathy but is nonetheless a singular manipulator. One might think that this type of person couldn't possibly exist. Logic would seem to dictate that in order to control the emotions of others one must personally have the capacity for compassion. But maybe she thinks this because she comes from a culture that values compassion so highly, more highly than anywhere else, a culture that has lost touch with the fact that in certain contexts compassion becomes a danger, it can undermine you, sometimes it must even be shut off. Certain people, she among them, do so because they must, otherwise their suffering is too great. Certain others, such as him, have never experienced compassion and this behooves them. With Il pulito she has understood that on a deeper level a person can be deaf to what others are feeling, but still have an advanced knowledge of what makes people tick, because they have noted the reactions of others and have understood how they respond to various stimuli. Such a person has fashioned their unconscious internal algorithms accordingly, refined that type of software. Il pulito could never have been Il pulito if he'd had empathy. Then a great many actions would have been impossible for him to perform because of their inherent cruelty. He would have excluded the possibility of those actions, unconsciously, because that's how empathetic people work. They don't even consider certain things, they exclude them, never knowing what it is that they are excluding.

It's because of his singular talent for manipulation that she must not, under any circumstance, read his messages. She is strong only so long as she does not read what he's writing. Like Orpheus in Hades, she must not turn back, no matter what the voices are saying. So no looking at her cell phone. One, two, three. *First things first.* Now she's grocery shopping. After that she'll go home and stay far away from her phone. She'll only pick it up to communicate with Ben and maybe, if all goes to plan, with his friends. Everything will go well. She hasn't had any contact with Il pulito for several days now. She's through the darkest part of the tunnel and there's a chance that this will indeed go well, that she's heading for the end of the tunnel now, that she will get free, that almost all of Hades is behind her and she's starting to see the light ahead. Mythology, that battery of lofty sacrosanct legends hewn by men, needs to be rewritten. She could give it a try, if only for her own purposes. In her story, she will be the first to be tested, but will resist the whispers. She will be the first not only to see the light after the long walk through the darkness but also the first to step out into it, bathe in it, be enveloped by it, and finally be liberated.

Such are her thoughts.

HOW DOES ONE go about finding traces of a person's friends in that person's home? Ben is hardly the kind of man who holds on to people's business cards. She roots around, knowing it's unseemly, but well, it is what it is. The paranoid multilingual repetitions occur ever more often, she knows it's a sign of stress, every language in her brain has to be gone through and if she finds herself at a loss for words, she has to stop and look them up. She doesn't want the languages to start disappearing, dissolving, melting, and calving like massive icebergs from her interior. Without those icebergs, without her languages, she is nobody. She must stem these repetitions and thoughts, because all thoughts lead to Il pulito. Stop. She has to stop. Focus on the task. *Concentrati sul compito.* Invite Ben's friends over. Make a little life, make arrangements, think other thoughts. While rooting around Ben's house, she finds women's effects. Necklaces, lipstick, a G-string, a mild intimate soap that she can't imagine belongs to Ben. But she's not about to blow this out of proportion. Will not hold him accountable, will not make a scene. Now it's only a matter of staying the course. Surely the soap is from an ex he used to live with. Has he ever lived with a woman? They haven't talked about it. They've barely talked about anything. But of course Ben has had live-in girlfriends. He's in his forties. Besides, whoever is out with the net must accept the catch. She looks around the living room. He appears to have lived here for a while. There are piles all over the place, as happens when a person has lived in a small space for a long time. She pulls books out of a bookcase, peers in. All sorts of things have fallen behind them. Pieces of tape, an old pen, a calculator. She concludes that he has lived here for at least ten years. Just to have a theory, something to go on. Ben has lived in this house for at least ten years. If you've lived in a house for ten years, there's a good chance you know your neighbors. She stands at the window that faces the house opposite and looks out. A man is working on a car in the driveway. The hood is up and he's tinkering with his tools. He has a scarf tied around his head and is wearing dirty jeans. He looks like Bruce Springsteen. She takes a deep breath, steels herself. She smooths her hair with one hand and clears her throat. He looks like an American version of someone from her village, which is good, she knows how to talk to people like that. Then she strides out the front door, across the street, and onto the neighbor's property.

"Hello," she says, holding out her hand. "I'm Ben's girlfriend."

She stands there with her hand outstretched. The man doesn't take it, but holds up a greasy hand by way of apology.

"My my, Ben's girlfriend," he says, wiping his hand on his jeans. "How about that. What's on your mind, *sugar*?"

"I was thinking of throwing a party," she says.

"A party?"

"A surprise party for Ben."

The man smiles a smile she can't interpret.

"Is that so?"

"Yes."

He laughs. Then he says, "Oh Lord. Oh Lord."

She doesn't understand this *Oh Lord* business. But she persists: "So I need help getting in touch with his closest friends. About six or seven of them. You're invited too, if you consider yourself to be among them, that is."

"Seven or so, and I'm invited too?" He laughs. "Sounds nice."

As he smiles, he checks out her breasts and lets his gaze drift on down, over her waist and thighs. He clearly enjoys chasing tail. Best to get right to it.

"Can you help me out? Do you have some sort of grapevine, can you get in touch with them, invite them?"

"Sure thing. If there's free grub, people will turn up."

"Yep. Free grub. Seven o'clock."

"I'll see you then, *sugar.*"

She turns around, walks down the driveway and into Ben's house. She goes back to the window and watches Bruce continue his work on the car. That went better than expected, she thinks. That truly went better than expected. If everyone comes who Bruce said will come, it will have gone so much better that she'd have to suspect the demon had a hand in it. But she must put such thoughts out of mind. She has a plan, and now it's time to follow through.

She cooks all afternoon. She chops, browns, boils, and makes salads. They start dropping in, one by one, a little absentmindedly. First Bruce, who's wearing the same stained trousers as when he was tinkering with the car, but at least he seems to have washed his hands. He winks at her and holds up a hand. More people arrive, women and men. They help themselves to peanuts from the bowl she has set out and toss them into the air to catch them in their mouths, and if the occasional nut falls on her freshly vacuumed carpet, they do not bend down to pick it up. No one is dressed up and she's in her best finery, a slightly sheer dress from a luxury boutique in Florence and a slip that gets staticky and clings to her skin in a nice way. Every other woman in the room is more attractive than she is. She is the most done up and the least attractive of all. She feels unbelievably foolish. Like a Maypole: adorned and in the center, but no one is talking to you. Eventually as many as nine people have arrived, and they keep coming, people who are coming because the ones who are already there seem to be sending messages about free grub or something else, she doesn't know, but soon there are at least fifteen people in Ben's little house. Everyone is walking on the wall-to-wall carpet with their dirty shoes, some even go into Ben's kitchen and open the doors and cabinets without asking first. The stew she made is sputtering on the stove. Someone grabs a plate and starts piling on the antipasto. The buffalo mozzarella quickly disappears and she has to take more bottles of wine out of the fridge. This is not how she had imagined it. They were supposed to turn up and stand around talking to her, they would get to know each other, drink some bubbly, and then Ben would come home and see them all there, and he'd be surprised. Surprised, but happy. He'd see that she carries with her no trace of social anxiety. More people drop in and she loses count. But she shouldn't be petty. It's getting out of hand and she doesn't know what to do, but whatever she does, she shouldn't stoop to pettiness. She thinks she should just play it cool, sometimes things don't turn out the way you planned, you have to go with it. But it hardly helps that her English seems to have gone to the dogs all of a sudden. When she opens her mouth it's as if she has adopted Il pulito's southern Italian accent. Many of the people coming into Ben's house ignore her, and if they don't, they start looking around for someone else after a quick chat. The affair is turning out to be an utter failure, there is no other way to put it. The kitchen is teeming with people, all helping themselves to her food. And they're just eating, they're not even commenting on how tasty it is. The cultural differences between Florence and New Orleans seem titanic. Here, you just *are*, and it's all good; it must be the air, the heat combined with the humidity, making everything lose its contours and become unruly. She has to do something. She has to take control of the situation. So she'll make a fool of herself. So she'll appear strange, she's from a different culture after all, and so you do nutty things. "Receive me kindly, stranger that I am," isn't that what Sebald said? Couldn't they just do the same here, understand that if she's making a fool of herself now it's because they do things differently where she's from, *otra manera de lei, otro modo donde ella* . . .

She plants herself in the middle of the crowded living room, bangs a knife against her glass.

"*Hi folks, truly, I am so happy you are all here, I really wanted to do somethi—*"

A man shouts: "Can someone turn on the music?"

She's about to take back the floor when music starts pouring from the speakers, so loud that it's impossible for her to make herself heard. It's a rap song with someone yelling *Fuck you!* rhythmically and at regular intervals, *Fuck you! Fuck you!* People are rocking back and forth and some are singing along—singing?—no, they're not singing, they're *roaring* with their clenched fists in the air, *Fuck you! Fuck you!*

She takes refuge in the bedroom and shuts the door behind her. Oh God. What has she done? Why is she even here? She feels so incredibly far away. The iron claw has again grabbed hold of her heart and she misses Il pulito so much that her legs begin to quake. Mickey, Mickey, Mickey. What have I done?

She picks up her phone. No new messages from Ben. He'll be coming home to this chaos. Though they're his friends, so maybe he'll manage to get through to them, tell them that she's his girlfriend from Europe, she meant well but it turned out wrong. Playing hostess to a bunch of people she doesn't know, idiotic, sure, but sometimes a person does idiotic things and now it's done so she has to bite the bullet, put up with the situation, and focus on *damage control*. She'll go back out there soon. To a living room full of strangers and music blaring *Fuck you* on repeat. Maybe she should down some liquor and start screaming too, but she can't, doesn't know how. She'll go back out soon and find a way to blend in. But first she's just going to check Il pulito's messages. She has to. She can't help it, sitting on your hands doesn't help, everything is happening of its own accord now. She can't resist, she can't, not in this situation where back is the only way. The magnetic force is too strong and she is only human. She takes her phone, opens the app, sees Il pulito and the black dot indicating that there are unread messages. She opens them and starts reading. She reads hungrily, lustily, thirstily, lapping up the words as if she were wandering in the desert and his words were the last drops of water after a rain.

HAND TREMBLING, SHE puts the phone down. It's as if for the past few minutes (hours?) she was sucked out of the house, out of the city, out of Louisiana, and out of the United States, right into something else, a vortex of hunger, agony, suffering, and pain. By turns there were tears, images of Il pulito's swollen red face streaked with tears, by turns threats and photos of him with the now empty vodka bottle from the fridge and a towering bridge behind him, *I'm throwing myself off, Minnie, how will you live with yourself knowing that you killed Mickey?* And later the anger and threats caused by her failure to respond. *Stronza, troia, a scopare tutti, puttana.* And then the pleas. *I love you and I'm an idiot, but I'm your idiot, sono il tuo coglione, only you can heal me and only you can get me to be a good person.* It's a roller-coaster ride through an inky darkness, all the while she's thinking that her heart is about to burst. She should die now, there is no other possible end to this cellular feed. It's what she deserves, for leaving him like that, what he said was true, they're both so broken, they have to help each other, they're sick, they can't handle the outside world, all they can do is lean on each other and help each other forward, the lame leading the blind, the mute leading the deaf, love cannot be restrained, it can grow out of anything, like flowers can grow from cracks in the asphalt, love can grow from the cracks of violence . . . She deserves his punishment and she craves it. Only his punishment can heal her now. He will hurt her, but he will not kill her. It's his protective instinct, she can trust it, lean into it, there's an ancient balance and she can be weak and everything can be brought to a head, but she won't die because he doesn't want her to die, not if they can be together. And there's no doubt that she deserves her punishment. She has left Il pulito and Il pulito has been through hell because of her, meanwhile she's been lying in Ben's bed, waiting for him to get over his aversion and take her in his arms. Il pulito has gone through all the torments of hell and he has sought her out like a blind man seeks a warm body in the night, only to find iciness and deceit, because that's what she's like, beyond the shadow of a doubt, she is ice-cold and deceitful. She thinks of his toes again and her chest tightens, the sudden tenderness suffocates her. She must call him. But when did he send his most recent message? Two days ago. So he hasn't texted her in two whole days . . . What does that mean? Has he given up? Has he killed himself? Has he found another woman, has he gone to a *casa rurale* with some ravishing female colleague? The last message he sent, however, was not a suicide note. It was a brief *Call me. Please call me.* It calms her for the moment, to the extent that she is able to think *first things first* and, with that phrase in her head, put down her phone, and go back out to the living room.

She can sense that something is off as she makes her way across Ben's bedroom to get to the door, but she can't pinpoint what it is. The second she puts her hand on her doorknob, it hits her. It's the silence. She listens and yes, it's dead silent. It's silent out there, dead silent in the living room. No music, no one talking loudly, no one roaring *Fuck you!* or clattering around with Ben's plates.

Jerking her hand away from the knob as if it were burning hot, she whispers to herself, "What the hell?"

What happened? Why didn't she hear anything, hear them all leaving? They didn't even say *goodbye?* Was she so engrossed in Il pulito's messages that she shut off her ears? How utterly out of character. But yes, there is silence. Deafening silence. No one talking in a normal conversational tone, no one moving around. She looks out the window. The necklaces are still swaying in the neighbor's tree, but no wind can be heard. She takes a deep breath, pushes down on the handle, and leaves the room.

The guests are gone, but for one. A woman. She's sitting, legs crossed, in an armchair that has been dragged away from its place by the coffee table. It has been turned toward the bedroom door, in her direction, and the woman's eyes are fixed on the door as she comes out. The woman looks as if she has spent a very long time sitting there, waiting. The expanse of dirty carpet around her, strewn with potato chips and plates. She even thinks she sees a smoldering cigarette. The woman's hands are on the armrests and her chin is tilted slightly down, the woman is looking up at her darkly. She glances around the room to see if Ben is there. He isn't. She pauses, then crosses the threshold and shuts the door behind her.

"Where is everyone?" she says in as normal a tone as she can muster.

"Gone," says the woman.

"Since when?"

The woman doesn't answer.

"All right," she says and clears her throat. "And who are you?"

"Jennifer."

Jennifer. She wants to ask why Jennifer hasn't left along with all the others, but she doesn't feel that she can pose the question.

"Sit down," Jennifer says.

She pulls up a chair and sits down, still feeling dizzy from Il pulito's many messages. She makes an effort to sit up straight with her hands on her knees. Jennifer looks her up and down.

Eventually Jennifer asks, "Can you explain what all this is? What you're up to?"

It feels like the blood is freezing in her veins. She wasn't expecting this tone, the deep contempt it conveys. What does this woman mean?

"Explain yourself," Jennifer reiterates. "Who are you, and why have you thrown a party here at Ben's?"

She draws a breath, slowly begins to explain, saying that she met Ben in Florence and they've been together ever since. Jennifer asks for how long, and she replies, "A few weeks."

"*Together?*" Jennifer says. "Do you mean together, like a couple?"

"Yes," she says, "or no, I don't know…"

"You had sex?"

"Yes. But…" The sentence is left hanging.

"But?" says Jennifer.

"But he hasn't wanted me since I got here. He hasn't touched me since I came to New Orleans."

Jennifer nods slowly, not once taking her eyes off her. Slowly, the suspicion that something is terribly wrong creeps in. Something is wrong, something is out of whack, she can read it in Jennifer's face, in its dogged, vaguely threatening expression. There is something underlying, something that could be released at any moment and take a swat at her, like a dragon's tail.

"You're not his type," Jennifer says.

She shrugs, tries to stay calm. She checks the time. Ben will turn up soon, he has to. Talking to this woman is pointless. Jennifer has already decided that she doesn't like her and isn't about to change her mind, she can't do anything about it. It feels unfair not to be given the benefit of the doubt. Still, she has no choice but to try and keep her balance in this situation.

She'll have to say something. A person can't sit in silence forever. She has to say something, because the silence has become unbearable.

So she says, "Okay. So, who are you then?"

She doesn't actually want to ask this question, because she can guess the answer. Jennifer is Ben's partner. And something has gone wrong between them, they were living together, but it went wrong, and he went to Europe for a while to get some space. In this space, he met her and what happened in Florence should have stayed in Florence, but instead he made the mistake of inviting her here and she, in turn, made the mistake of accepting his invitation. A series of events that could have gone right—or at least had a shot at staying within the bounds of normalcy—have gone wrong.

The delay in reply confirms her suspicions. Jennifer keeps holding her tongue while looking at her coldly. Her own gaze roves across the living room and to the plot across the way, trying to see if Bruce is outside with the car. He isn't. She squirms in her chair, thinks of Il pulito. She lived in a crazy bubble with Il pulito. It's true. She lived in a crazy bubble with Il pulito and now she has fled the bubble, she has managed to make her way through that sticky, resistant membrane, and she has reentered the world only to find that the world can be even crazier than the bubble. It's like that Kusturica film, where people in a Bosnian shelter think that the war is still going on above them, but in fact the war ended long ago and by the time they manage to get out, it's a new era and a new war has begun, and then they think that sure, everything was crazy down in the cellar but it's much worse out here. That's what this is like for her. That's exactly what it's like.

She tries to read the thoughts behind Jennifer's eyes. The silence is viscous, as if it were composed of something that would soon coat her skin and smother her.

"I have to go to the bathroom," she says at last.

"You're staying put until I decide what to do with you," Jennifer replies.

"What are you going to do with me?" she asks.

"Well. Let me think."

This just keeps getting crazier and crazier. She wants to get her phone, to read through Il pulito's messages again. She hasn't had a chance to process everything he's written, she's still in shock.

Jennifer picks up a piece of popcorn from the carpet, throws it at her, and laughs. She has a hard time taking this in. A strange woman just threw *popcorn* at her. Hello? Where am I? Can I wake up now, please? Despite the absurdity of the situation, she feels her throat constrict with fear. Yes, now she can feel it, clearly, how afraid she is of this woman. A second piece of popcorn lands on her.

Her voice feeble, she says, "Would you stop doing that? Can't we just talk?"

Threat is in the air. So far just a hint, indistinct at that, but it's there, like a whiff of something acrid among other aromas. A premonition, a tremor foreboding a quake. In a flash, she turns to one of the living-room windows and calls out: "Ben!"

The echo ebbs between the walls and is followed by a dense silence. Jennifer stands up and slowly walks over to her. Jennifer is now standing so close that she can smell the fabric softener in the woman's jeans.

"Ever since I first saw you earlier today, I've wanted to smack your meddling little mug."

Okay. A provocation. Swim by. If you swim with your barbs retracted, nothing can grab hold of you.

"I see," she says. "Why?"

In lieu of an answer, Jennifer grabs her by the hair, yanks her face up, and gives her a hard slap. Her hand is like a branding iron on her cheek. Her scalp aches from the firm grip. She tears up. When Jennifer lets go of her, she looks away, stares down at the floor, blinking hard until the tears disperse.

"What the hell," she says, "what are you doing, what have I done to you?"

Jennifer just smiles at her.

"I can't stay here," she says. "I'm leaving."

She stands up and goes to the bedroom to get her handbag.

But then Jennifer follows after her, grabs her arm and holds it tight.

"You're staying with me."

"I'm going out to find Ben."

"You're not going anywhere. You're just gonna be cool and do as I say."

In retrospect, she'll regret her disobedience. She could have simply sat back down on the chair, simply sat there and maybe tried to doze off a little, waited for Ben to arrive, not provoked Jennifer. That's what she could have done, de-escalated, she knows how, she has done it thousands of times with Il pulito. She could have sat there and let Jennifer throw popcorn from the carpet at her until she got bored, or until Ben arrived. She could have made herself invisible for a few hours, she knows how to do that too, how to appear to be thinking about something else so that the people around you relax and start thinking about something other than the state you're in, allowing the threads to lose their tension, so that the beast supervising you thinks you're calm and it might even fall asleep at its post. Had she done so, everything might have gone well. Instead, it is her resistance that gives rise to the situation, goading Jennifer, which makes it impossible to rewind the cassette tape.

"You're not the boss of me," she says.

"No?" Jennifer says. "Are you sure?"

The anger rises in her, the barbs protrude.

"I'm leaving," she says.

She gets up and heads for Ben's bedroom.

"Who do you think you are?" Jennifer calls after her.

"Who do I think I am?" she says. "I'm Ben's girlfriend, and you're an intruder that he lost interest in a long time ago and doesn't want to be with. He chose me. Do you understand? He chose me. *Me, me, me.*"

Something in Jennifer explodes; she lunges at her, flings her to the floor, and starts punching her in the face.

"You sick whore!" she screams. "You shoulda done your homework before you jumped into bed with him, you know as well as I do how men can be, you have to suss these things out before you get involved! You didn't and now you're gonna pay, you perverted little slut!"

She lies still and takes the beating. Her anger vanishes and she feels genuine fear, so much fear that her body freezes up. This woman doesn't know how to fight, she thinks, and it's dangerous being beaten by someone who doesn't know how to fight. Il pulito knew how to stop shy of killing her but this woman doesn't, she can tell by the nature of the blows, this woman doesn't know how, she could kill her at any second, by mistake. She wishes it were Il pulito beating her. Il pulito's familiar old punches, Il pulito who loved her but couldn't handle his anger, suddenly there's safety in those punches of his, none of this uncontrolled violence from a perfect stranger. Then everything goes black. It's like falling into a velvet pit. The pain disappears, the fear disappears, and darkness closes around her like the soft walls of a hot mouth.

IN THE DARKNESS she remembers. She remembers her childhood, when she was five. Her mother was crying in the living room. Her mother was crying on the sofa, and as for her, she was standing on the floor feeling the horror spread through her body, because she had never seen her mother cry before and understood that something very serious must have happened for this to come to pass. Something on par with the ground cracking open during an earthquake or icy hail lashing down from a midsummer sky. Her father was beside her. There they stood, side by side, she and her father, looking at her mother. It was then she realized that her father was at a loss as well, and so the grip of fear tightened around her. Her mother kept crying, and her father remained unsure of how to comfort her. Finally he turned to her and said, "Let's go into town and do some shopping, and then Mom can have some peace and quiet."

They drove to the city center and he parked in the Konsum parking lot. They went into the grocery store, but her father wasn't shopping, they were just wandering the aisles. Eventually they walked back out, passing the registers without making a purchase. Right before the parking lot, at the entrance to the shopping center, they spotted a large yellow plastic rabbit, a coin-operated ride. She asked her father if she could ride the rabbit. Her father put in a coin and the rabbit took speed. She laughed out loud for her father, she squealed, because the ride was so much fun, but her father wasn't looking at her. So her laughter slowly died. She sat joylessly on the bounding rabbit, eyes on her father's sad back. He seemed to be staring straight into the sunset, straight into the bright yellow light that at this time of day was setting the parking lot aflame.

NOW TOO SHE awakens in the light, a bright yellow light directed at her face. She opens her eyes and squints into it. A lamp is shining on her and there they are, behind the light, Ben and Jennifer. She is so relieved to see him. Ben the Savior. He saved her from Il pulito, now he will save her from this woman, from this stark raving mad Jennifer. Or simply explain that she shouldn't be angry with her, she hasn't done anything wrong, it's all a misunderstanding.

"Ben," she whispers, reaching for him.

But he doesn't receive her, he just stands there with a worried look on his face.

"How are you?" he says.

"Fine," she says, though her head feels strange, dizzy and sore, possibly swollen.

"You've taken a few blows to the head," Ben says.

The lamp is turned away from her face and Ben nods to Jennifer, who is clearing her throat.

"Jennifer wants to say something," he says, gesturing toward her.

But Jennifer says nothing.

"Jen," Ben says. "What was it you that were going to say?"

Jennifer clears her throat again and says, "I'm sorry. I just got so angry." She pauses. "You see," she continues, "it's like this. Ben belongs to me, and you showed up at an inopportune time. I can't have another woman in my man's house. I can't. He's mine, and sometimes he gets it in his head that he should enjoy a freedom he doesn't have. You're one of his mistakes and that's his fault, but you're at fault too."

"But I didn't know he was taken," she says. "How could I have known?"

"You could have asked him," Jennifer says.

"I did," she says.

"You should have asked twice," Jennifer says. "That's what I meant earlier. You should have asked more carefully, pressed the point. Snooped around."

She looks at Ben. He doesn't say a word.

"Aren't you going to say anything?" she says. "You're the liar here."

But Ben offers no more than a slow shrug and looks uncertainly at Jennifer.

"He's just a man," says Jennifer. "You can't really have high hopes as far as honesty goes."

"But doesn't he have to take responsibility for—"

"Don't piss me off again," Jennifer says. "Don't play dumb. You, me, and every other woman around knows this, and didn't you have someone else over there too, some fat fucking guy in Europe, Ben told me about how you'd walk around holding hands in the evenings and how you cheated on him with Ben, so don't come here and play dumb. You took Ben because he served a purpose for you at the time. You *used* him."

She doesn't want to trigger Jennifer's rage again so she nods and says *Whatever*, she doesn't care, she just wants to get out of here. Jennifer can have Ben and the house, the whole shebang, she doesn't care, she wants to go back to Europe now, to Italy, to Florence, and she'll only prevail upon them to call her taxi to the airport, so she can catch the first flight to London. She looks at them, but they don't answer.

"Okay?" she says. "Can you do that, can you call me a taxi?"

They stare at the floor.

"Ben?" she says. "Can you at least do that for me, arrange a taxi?"

Ben seems distressed, looks between her and Jennifer, and shakes his head as if he doesn't know what to say.

"The thing is, Minnie . . ."

She doesn't understand. What's going on? A taxi, how hard can it be! If they'd just help her with that, then they could call it even, she won't bother them anymore, she's leaving, going away, to Europe, to her home country, or no, to Italy, Il pulito's home country, but since Il pulito is hers, his country is a bit hers as well. She doesn't say this last thing but she thinks it and she almost smiles at the thought because she is reminded of *her* man. *Sono un coglione*, he used to say, *ma sono il tuo coglione. I'm an idiot, but I'm your idiot.* Now she's going home to him, her very own idiot.

It's Jennifer who breaks the silence. She fetches a mirror, which she holds up to her. In the mirror, she sees her battered face. It's worse than she thought. She has two puffy black eyes. Her hair is sticky with half-coagulated blood. Her lip is swollen too, and split.

"You do understand that you can't get on a plane looking like that," Jennifer says.

"I don't care," she says, "I can travel naked, black and blue if I have to, I don't care."

Jennifer squirms. "But other people might," she says.

"Who?"

"The police."

Yes but she's not going to the police! She's going home. Sure, they get that, but what if she changes her mind at the airport? Once she's there and through security, she might realize that what Jennifer did wasn't very nice, and then she might go to the police, who have an office there at customs, and snitch. That would be no good for Jennifer, because she's on parole and would be locked back up if the police found out.

"No, no," she says. "I won't do that."

She would never, she swears. Jennifer looks a little ashamed and Ben refuses to meet her eye.

"Sure, you're making promises now," Jennifer says, "because you're starting to get scared of what we might do to you otherwise, the power is in our hands, as it were, but we can't be *certain*. We don't know you from Adam, after all. We don't know what might occur to you. And the police in New Orleans aren't like the police in other places. The police here are *sick fuckers*."

But what do they mean? She almost bursts out laughing, because this is the most absurd thing she's ever experienced. So what are they going to do? They can't hold her against her will. Well yes, they can actually, Jennifer says, her tone almost silky smooth. That's exactly what they can do. They can keep her hidden until her face has gone back to normal and the evidence is gone. Hidden? Hidden how? Is she not going to be allowed outside? Precisely, and not only that, she can't stay here with Ben because this is Ben and Jennifer's house, they'll have to move her to Jennifer's stepfather's old house, which is a ways outside the city and is as good as abandoned; her stepfather checks on the place from time to time, that's it. She'll have to stay there until her face is back to normal. She stares at them.

"You can't be serious," she says gruffly, "this can't be. What if something happens to me out there, an abandoned house in this city, that's putting someone like me in mortal danger, I come from another continent with a different bacterial flora and—"

Jennifer shrugs, chuckles. "Well, *bitch*, that's your problem."

SITTING IN THE backseat of Jennifer's car, she's still thinking that this isn't happening. Is she asleep? Is she asleep in Il
pulito's apartment and dreaming of escape? Of having committed the insane act of leaving him, traveling all the way to
New Orleans, installing herself at Ben's, and throwing the
party where she was beaten up by Ben's girlfriend? Of talking to a man who she decided was named Bruce, and who she
kept an eye out for as they marched her to Jennifer's car, but
only his car with its propped-open hood was to be seen? This
is too sick to be true, she thinks, it can only be a dream. She
opens her eyes as wide as she can to see if this wakes her up.
She doesn't wake up. She's still in the car with Jennifer and
Ben. She dearly wishes she could wake up under the wooden
ceiling in Il pulito's apartment. At any moment between
their visit to la dottoressa and her leaving for the airport.
Right there, in those days. When Il pulito had turned himself
around, when he'd come up with the idea of them getting their
heads screwed on straight and booked an appointment with
la dottoressa, when they'd had one session and she could still
stop the flow of events and make sure they go there one more

time, apologize to la dottoressa for the insults, stop talking about demons, start doing regular sessions with la dottoressa and try to sort everything out, become sane, become normal people, the two of them. But as much as she wants to wake up, she doesn't. She's still sitting in Ben's girlfriend's car, on her way to Ben's girlfriend's stepfather's abandoned house.

They're driving along the Mississippi. A wide, brown river, big ships stacked with containers. You don't imagine it being this wide, but it is. They drive alongside the ships and she hears them sounding their horns, long and slow, resigned, as if the captain had nothing better to do en route than let his boat's lament ring out. The riverbank is scorched and graveled and there is trash everywhere. Large bridges crisscross the city. They drive on, perhaps half an hour, along what looks like an unmoving greenish lagoon. She sees swarms of insects in the air. Then it's as if there is an end to the moisture and the ground becomes as dry as dust, like a moonscape. She stops looking at the landscape and stares ahead. Jennifer has demonstratively wrapped her arm around Ben's backrest, is stroking his neck with her well-groomed fingers. She sees this, and she thinks she should be the one stroking his neck like that. If only she hadn't rocked the boat, if only she had played a different hand.

Then Ben slows the car down, drives up a dirt road, and then another, until they come to a gray shack. It's on a hill that looks like it's surrounded by garbage. A second shack stands right next to it, otherwise the area is uninhabited. In the distance is something that could be an old factory. A few hundred yards from the two shacks, the river flows, water thick, green and brown. She wonders what kind of animals live here.

Because that's always the way, this is as bad as it can be, you think, and then you realize that it can get much worse. She'd thought that the bat in Il pulito's apartment was as bad as it could get. Then she thought the cockroaches in Ben's house were the worst, until one night she woke up to a huge spider crawling across her shoulder. Now she thinks this situation is the worst she's ever been in. What will reveal itself next?

An older man is sitting on the shack's dilapidated porch. He's rocking in a rocking chair and a rifle is propped against the house behind him. Jennifer and Ben get out of the car and go up to the porch. She watches Jennifer turn around and point at her. The man shades his eyes with his hand and squints to catch a glimpse of her in the car. Jennifer waves her over.

"This is Hector," she says. "My stepdad. He's gonna take care of you."

She walks slowly toward the porch. She doesn't understand the situation. She's not from here, she's only been here a short while, she hasn't learned to interpret minor gestures and wordless exchanges.

"What the . . . ?" Hector says when he sees her bruised and battered face. "Jennifer, you weren't supposed to—"

"It just happened. She provoked me."

"A week or so should do it," says Ben. "Keep us posted and I'll come pick her up and drive her to the airport." He turns to her. "Bye, Minnie. Don't be afraid, no one's gonna hurt you here. I'm sorry the trip didn't turn out the way you'd hoped. I'll put your handbag in a cupboard in Hector's kitchen for safekeeping, and I'll bring the rest of your stuff another day. And one more thing. I'm fully aware that this is all my fault, but I'm going to make sure you get on your way as soon as you're better, all right?"

He quickly strokes her cheek. They lead her into Hector's kitchen, which is dirty and full of plates caked with leftovers. Hector appears with a chain, which they attach to a pole sticking out of the ground below the porch, and at the end of the chain they attach an iron ring, which they in turn fit around her ankle. She looks at Ben.

"This a joke, right? Isn't this a joke? You're actually chaining me up?"

Ben looks ashamed.

"At least it's a long chain," he says. "You can pretty much move around as you please in parts of the house and the property."

"'At least it's a long chain!' Are you hearing yourself?"

"It is what it is," he says, shrugging. "It is what it is."

"But we fell in love," she says. "Remember?"

It's no use. He merely shrugs and looks at her with resignation. She can read his gaze: If only she hadn't contacted his friends, everything would have been fine. If only she had played it cool, everything could have worked out. Then he squints at the porch, where Jennifer is still talking to her stepfather.

"Jen and I took a break," he says quietly. "We decided to stop seeing each other. We've had a hard time, just like you and that fatso in Florence. But then you opened Pandora's box, Minnie, and here we are . . ."

"You have to help me," she whispers. "Ben. You can't leave me here."

"I know," Ben says, holding up a hand as if to block her words. "I know. Let's wait until Jen calms down a bit and then I'll come back. I told you. I'll make sure you get home. I promise."

"Just you," she says. "Don't bring her. Come alone, help me get free, and drive me to the airport. Please, tonight if you can, because this place really does look dangerous."

"Nah, this isn't a dangerous place. Nothing can happen to you here."

"There might be animals."

"The animals aren't as dangerous as they look. You get used to it. Just take it easy and rest up, and I'll be back before you know it."

Jennifer comes walking toward them, whistles, and then she and Ben drive off.

The first night at Hector's, she sleeps on the porch. He sets out a stained mattress that stinks of old bodies. Whose? She wants know, but Hector doesn't say anything, he might as well be mute because he doesn't say a single word to her even though she's babbling on, asking him about all sorts of things. Who is he, how long has he lived here, how old is Jennifer, how long have Jennifer and Ben been together? She gets no answers. He just walks his thin, crooked body around, smoking, looking up at the ceiling, giving the wall a little kick, as if he were planning to renovate and trying to prioritize. It's hot. A damp heat that intensifies every smell, an intrusive heat that creeps inside your clothes and presses up against you.

She catches the stench of dirty river water.

"The river stinks like a drain," she tells Hector.

"The river *is* a drain," he replies with a dry laugh.

There is a toilet, but she's not allowed to use it. Only Hector is allowed to use it, and it's an earth closet, because the shack isn't connected to a sewage system and all the shit goes into a box under the floor. She is, however, given a bucket that is to be kept as far from the house as her chain will stretch. In it she is to do her business. She has never shat in a bucket before. It's a challenge, because you can't put your weight on the rim of the bucket; you have to flex your thigh muscles as hard as you can and get your sphincter to open at the same time. She sits on the ground until the pressure peaks, then in a flash hovers over the bucket. She must look ridiculous. If Hector is sitting somewhere inside watching her, he must be getting a good laugh. Maybe he's filming her and sending clips to Jennifer to show her how her rival is struggling to empty her bowels and then Jennifer might show it to Ben. She must not get paranoid. *Non cadere nella paranoia, no te caigas en la paranoia.* Does she care? Yes, she cares. She doesn't want to be made a fool of in front of Ben. But isn't that a lesser problem at this stage? Well yes, besides, it's nothing compared to how embarrassing it gets when Hector comes to fetch the bucket while holding his nose and making a face like it stinks, and he's not wrong, the stench reaches all the way to where she's sitting. She pees directly on the ground, because she knows from her childhood outhouse that urine and feces shouldn't mix because then it'll smell even worse. She tries to protect the sliver of dignity to which a captive who is made to shit in a bucket and pee on the ground can lay claim. The important thing is not to break down inside. If you do, you're screwed, if you snap, then one thing after the next will crumble. Her health, her face, her body. She has to think long-term, try to see what's happening now as a kind of hardship. When she's back in Europe, she'll make friends. Yes, she'll make friends if only to have someone with whom she can talk through what's happening to her now. She tries not to think about how good she actually had it with Il pulito, how paradise was within reach, if only she had fought for it, if only she had followed the road he wanted them to follow together. The road to mental health. *La via della salute mentale.* Or maybe you wouldn't call it the Road to Mental Health but at least it was a road, a possibility, which with time and great effort could take them to a good life. Why didn't she fight for it?

Night approaches. The temperature drops and a stubborn dampness slithers out of the river, slow and hissing like an old snake.

SHE WAKES UP to the warm sun on her face. Hector is pottering around the kitchen. She asks for water. After a while he brings her a bottle. She drinks and feels sick after, as if it wasn't pure water.

"Fresh from the river, right?" she says to Hector's mute back.

After a while she feels dizzy.

"What was in the bottle? Are you poisoning me? Please don't poison me, I don't want to die."

Soon she feels so faint she can hardly stand. She ends up languishing in the shade on the porch. For long periods she sits there without so much as a thought, that's the beauty of it, no thoughts, just the sound of Hector in the earth closet, banging away with tools and muttering to himself in Spanish. She wonders where his rifle is now and if her chain reaches into the kitchen, to the cupboard with her bag. She wonders if her cell phone is still in her bag. She doesn't feel hungry, but when Hector comes out with a can of cold white beans that he's stuck a fork into she wolfs it down. She doesn't like white beans in tomato sauce back home, but these go down

nicely and give her a fleeting sense of inner peace. The car-
bohydrate calm. She puts the can on the railing, and there it
stays because Hector doesn't come back to fetch it. The hours
pass. The river stinks, the sun burns. She gets thirsty and wonders if she is allowed to go inside, into the shack, where there
is shade, if she is allowed to be there even though Hector is
there. I'm already reasoning like a dog, she thinks. Wondering what I can and can't do, constantly watching for my jailer.
She goes inside. The chain reaches a good ways into the living
room, but the door to the bathroom has been shut, seeming
to signal that Hector doesn't want to be disturbed. She takes a
seat on the porch again. After a while, Hector comes out with
a bottle of liquor, sits a short distance away from her on the
porch, and drinks. She thinks that if he gets drunk and falls
asleep, she can sneak over, whack him over the head with the
bottle, and take the key to the chain from his belt loop. She
imagines breaking free and wonders where she would run to.
And which way. She sits there for a long time, looking in every
direction. It's a good thing she's not impulsive, or she might
have already tried to escape, without first deciding which way
to run. She will use her time as a captive to figure out exactly
what to do once she manages to get free. That Ben and Jennifer will return is by no means certain. They could let her
die and then throw her in the river or in the brown lagoon
they drove past on the way here. No one knows where she
is. To the right is the old industrial building, to the left the
river. Straight ahead is a shack like Hector's, and behind it?
She can't see because the chain doesn't reach that far. Which
way is downtown? It seems impossible to tell from where she

is, but something tells her that when she gets loose, she should be able to get there by following the river upstream.

On the horizon she sees the roofs of tall, modern buildings. Somewhere too is the sea, and between her and the sea: miles and miles of marsh and cypress swamps.

As the sun sets, Hector comes out with another opened can of white beans. He hands it to her and looks around, spots the previous can on the railing with the fork jutting out. He takes the fork and hands it to her. She wants to point out that it's dirty, he could at least wash it, but doesn't have it in her. He has also brought her a bottle of cloudy water. She drinks it and again feels a mix of nausea and drowsiness. She falls asleep on the putrid mattress. She dreams of the murderer from her childhood, standing perfectly still next to her mattress, looking down at her through those small, square glasses of his. Then in the dream he suddenly opens his mouth and lets out a roar. The roar is booming, it is impossible to imagine that a roar of such magnitude could fit inside a body as slim and ordinary as the murderer's, but the murderer roars and in the dream she realizes that it's not the murderer roaring, but something within, what he's harboring. She wakes in a sweat and hears the resounding blasts of a steamship on the river a few hundred yards away through the murk.

THREE DAYS PASS. Hector doesn't hurt her, but he doesn't help her either. Two cans of white beans a day is what she is given to eat. She tries not to get dramatic about it. All she's doing is sitting here until her face is back to normal. Then she'll go home. She needs a mirror. If she could get her hands on a mirror, she could estimate how much time she has left at the shack. Because they're going to let her go when the bruises have faded and the swelling on her face has gone down, right? Of course they are, because stashing her away like this is an inconvenience for them. She must cling to this conviction as long as she is in this nightmare, or else she won't be able to cope. They are going to return. *Verranno, vendrán.* She asks for a mirror, *specchio, espejo,* but Hector only responds with a dismissive wave, as if he doesn't understand what she's saying.

At some point in the evening of the third day, a light blue compact car comes up the driveway. At first she thinks it's Ben.

"Ben," she whispers. "Ben."

"That's not Ben," Hector says from the house.

"Then who is it?"

"Noma."

"And who is Noma?"

"The neighbor."

Her spirits drop when she sees an ancient woman open the passenger door and step out. She is so small, so crooked, and so brittle, as if she were made of paper that had gotten wet and then was quickly dried on high heat. After she gets out of the car, a man in the front seat reaches behind him to shut the door that Noma has left open. The man doesn't even look up at Hector's house, much less see her. The old woman staggers off toward the shack next door, which appears to be a homecoming. Getting help from a person who looks like that is out of the question. She realizes this. A bone-dry old woman with one foot in the grave. Hector and Noma don't greet each other. Hector has turned his head away, as if he couldn't stand the sight of his neighbor. Noma takes her time walking to her shack and closes the door behind her. Noma's house is silent until evening, when the old woman switches the radio on. Lying on the mattress, which Hector has moved into the living room, she suddenly hears the radio.

"Don't get any ideas," she hears Hector say from the bedroom. "You won't hear anything about a missing person. No one is looking for you."

"That's not what I was hoping for. Why would there be a missing person's report? I'm not missing. I'm only here for a few days."

Hector does not answer. She listens to the radio for a bit.

"What station is she listening to?" she asks.

"Night radio for the blind," Hector replies.

"Is Noma blind?"

"Practically."

She's listening through the window that won't shut properly. She hears the night radio, a man talking about books and interviewing writers. Every now and then she hears Noma working in her backyard. It sounds like she's moving pots and dragging heavy bags around. In the middle of the night. *En medio de la noche, in piena notte.* Of course, she thinks, if you're blind, the dark is one less factor to take into consideration. She takes a sip of the polluted water. It starts raining, even so Noma carries on in her backyard.

THE DIZZY SPELLS keep getting longer. She tries asking Hector questions. His Spanish suggests that he is from Mexico, but where in Mexico? She also wonders what he's adding to the water, if he's heard from Jennifer and Ben, if he knows when they're coming, and if he can arrange for a mirror or at least tell her what her face looks like. But Hector doesn't want to talk to her and responds to every question with that dismissive wave.

On the evening of the fourth day, she asks if she can go over to the property line and talk to Noma.

"She's crazy," says Hector.

"How crazy?"

"Completely."

"Why?"

"After Katrina. Some of the people who refused to be evacuated couldn't take it, it messed with their heads, and they were never the same. Her husband and son died, one was swept away by the floodwaters and got caught in a power line. Now she's always thinking that the end is nigh and another hurricane's about to blow in and wipe New Orleans off the map for good."

"So you know her?" she says.

"We've lived here for so long. Katrina destroyed everything, but we still live here."

"Why don't you talk to each other?"

"What are we gonna say?"

He does that dismissive wave again and goes into the bedroom.

But at night, when Hector is asleep and the night radio for the blind is on is on, she sneaks out and manages to get almost all the way to the property line. She is a little less dizzy because she has been avoiding the water all evening.

"Psst," she says once she reaches the property line. "Hey you, Noma!"

The old woman looks up from the pots and by the bright, blank gaze she turns to the sky, she knows Noma can't see her.

"I'm standing over here," she continues, "I'm staying here with Hector, he and his daughter are holding me captive, I need help, can you help me?"

Noma sits there with her empty, shining eyes and listens. Then she stands up, reaches out her hands, and starts walking, feeling her way along the fence.

"Here," she whispers. "I'm here. Come, please, come closer. They've chained me up and I can't go any farther than this."

Noma makes her way. From her house, you can still hear the night radio, a female writer is talking enthusiastically about a crime novel she has written. Finally, Noma reaches her.

"May I touch you?" she whispers.

Noma nods slowly, her glassy gaze to the sky, and holds out her aged hand. She takes it, wraps her hands around it, and when she feels the warmth of that birdlike hand, the warmth of another person's skin, she bursts into tears.

"They're holding me captive," she whispers between sobs, "and I have to get out of here, can you help me? Can you help me? Please say you—"

"One day the Mississippi will rise from its riverbed," Noma says.

"What are you saying?" she says.

"And then the whole city will be laid to waste." Noma's voice is metallic, monotone. "Everything will be underwater and in the swamp the dangers will grow, the dangers that will kill us in the end."

She swallows. Hector was right. Noma is crazy. She starts crying again.

"Yes, Noma," she says. "That's right. The dangers will kill us."

"Kill us," Noma says.

"Noma," she says, "do you have a phone? A cell phone? A cell phone I could borrow, I need to call my boyfriend in Italy and tell him to come get me—"

"The swamps have already swallowed up a whole lot, but they will swallow even more. The swamps. Home to reptiles, but also swollen corpses."

"Oh, dear God, please . . ."

Hope fails, and she starts crying again. Right as she is about to let go of Noma's hands and go back inside to that septic mattress, Noma pulls her hand from her grasp and places it on her cheek. She looks up in surprise. How does Noma know where her cheek is? The old woman strokes her face again and again.

"You have suffered," she says. "I can feel it, the suffering, and I feel your longing. But even you will find peace when the apocalypse comes."

The tears return, falling harder now, as if this mad, prophetic sympathy has unleashed them. It starts raining. Water pummels mud. She and Noma stay put. Noma still and with the hint of a smile but not a word. They stand there in the rain, in the soupy mud, and soon the moment will reach its end, she thinks, because Hector will wake up and hear them, and then he will yank the chain and she'll have to go inside and lie back down on the mattress. But until that happens, she wants to stand here, feeling the touch of a fellow human being, a fellow human being who may seem insane but a human being nonetheless with warm hands, a voice, and words.

"I have to call my boyfriend," she says again. "I have to call Mickey."

"Mickey," Noma says. "You will call Mickey and Mickey will come."

"Exactly. When Mickey finds out I'm being held captive here, he'll be on the first plane across the Atlantic, and then he'll rent a car and get here in the blink of an eye, if I could just get my hands on a phone, a cell phone."

"Mickey," Noma repeats. "Mickey will show up in a car."

"Yes, exactly," she says, "Mickey. Mickey, my boyfriend. Who I have a stormy relation with."

She says *stormy relation*, but doesn't know if that's how to say it in English.

"*Stormy*," says Noma.

"Yes, exactly, stormy."

"*Winds*," says Noma. "*I know about winds.*"

"What are you saying?"

"*Winds. I know about winds. You know about winds. You will know about winds.*"

Oh, dear God. What kind of person is this?

"Noma, you can hear what I'm saying, you're not completely crazy, you're hearing me, you can help me, you have to help me, do you have a telephone?"

"*We all know about winds.*"

"Noma, it's like this. Listen. Please, listen. A demon moved into me, I'm sure of it, and another one moved into Mickey. It sounds crazy, but that's exactly what happened. Together, these demons set off all the winds of the world and we were dragged into them. Now I'm sitting here and the demon has fallen silent, doesn't speak, it's as if it's gone and that's why I have to get back to Mickey, because the demons are gone now, we might have a chance to..."

She stops speaking. She realizes how twisted this all sounds.

Then Noma says clearly, "The demon is not gone. It's waiting."

"What?" she says.

"It's not gone. Your demon. It's waiting."

"What do you mean 'waiting'? The demon thing was just a thing I said, a thought I have, what do you know about it, can you sense it, what do you mean?"

"When the apocalypse comes, we'll all find peace."

She thinks she's going crazy too, as if Noma's madness were contagious. But she needs clarity, she has to find out what Noma means by "the demon." Noma turns around and starts walking toward her shack.

"Noma, please, talk to me, help me . . . !" She stands in the mud and whimpers, pathetic, beside herself. "Noma, please, I beg . . ."

She lies down on the ground, lets her forehead sink into the soggy earth. It's over. She fought, often thinking she was getting somewhere, but now it's over. Over, here on some deserted patch of land in New Orleans, a place as good as any. As she's about to fall asleep in the mud, she feels Noma's hand on her head. It's a small hand, cool, still it feels warm because the rain is so cold.

"The demon in you," Noma whispers through the rain, "wants to get to the demon in him. It's the demon from whom you should seek help. You are weak, but the demon is strong. Let the demon help you get to Mickey."

WHEN SHE WAKES up the next morning, lying in the wet lukewarm mud, the sun beating down on her, she thinks that it must have been a dream. There's no way that she actually experienced what she's now remembering, it must be one of her bizarre dreams. She sits up and looks at Noma's house. It looks like no one has been there for ages. She looks up at Hector's house and there too it looks as if no one has been for ages. She stands up, staggers over to the porch, and sinks down against the wall in the shade. She thinks through what Noma said about the demon. Or was it something someone said in the dream? Does Noma exist? She looks toward Noma's shack. Hector comes out. She conducts an experiment. Half reclined against the porch wall, she imagines that she is drifting away, drifting deep inside herself, and as she does her instrument panel is being left unattended, so to speak. She lets the demon emerge, invites the demon to take the stage, the helm, the wheelhouse, she offers the demon to take the whole thing over, the whole ship of her, the whole situation here with Hector, here in New Orleans. And as she's thinking this, she hears herself say, "One day the river will rise from its bed and lay waste to us all."

She sees Hector flinch. He looks at her closely and for the first time she senses something in his gaze, if not terror then at least concern. He casts a glance at Noma's house, which looks shuttered and vacant.

"Do you want some water?" he says.

"Do you want me to have water?" she replies in the same rhythm of speech.

Hector goes into the shack and soon comes out with water. It's cold, he must have taken it from the fridge. It's a sign of certain respect, being given cold clean water instead of water that's lukewarm, poisoned. She drinks.

"You're poisoning me, aren't you, Hector?" she says once she has drunk it all up. "You and Jennifer. You think you can poison me. You can. Of course you can poison me. You can kill me in lots of ways, poisoning is just one of them."

She takes a break before continuing.

"But you have to remember one thing: There is a demon living inside of me, and that demon is stronger than I am. I am its host and it is my parasite, but it's not just any parasite. It will always find a way to survive. It will find a new host, and that host could very well be you, Hector. Or Jennifer. You wouldn't want Jennifer to be possessed by a demon, would you?"

Hector does his usual dismissive wave, but his face is tense. He doesn't like her talking this way. She smiles to herself. And the more she notices that he doesn't like it, the more pleasure she takes in continuing.

"The demon is hungry, Hector," she says, a little sing-songy. "Hungry, Hector, hungry ... *El demonio tiene hambre, Hector, quiere comer ...*"

"There's no such thing as demons," he mumbles.

"You don't even believe that yourself." She laughs. "Demons exist, and they are drawn to this place. I can sense them, I could sense them even before I came here, when I was walking around Ben's neighborhood, the chill between the buildings, cold drafts disappearing into the darkness between the houses."

Hector looks at her for a long time, then shakes his head and turns around, walks into the house. She sits tight out there. Time passes slowly and to occupy herself she starts singing. At first she's just humming. Then: *There is a house in New Orleans, they call the Rising Sun, and it's been the ruin of many a poor boy and God I know I'm one.* Her voice sounds weak and shaky, as brittle as ever, but when she notices that she knows the words, even though she knows she doesn't actually know the words, because she's never sung this song, only heard it, never dove into the lyrics, but when she notices the lyrics coming anyway, she raises her voice and sings even louder. Finally she's singing so loudly that she has to laugh between lyrics, because it sounds so twisted, rings so false, and yet she's doing this, yes, she's doing this, she's singing this song at the top of her lungs, filtering the words through her madness. *Oh, mother, tell your children, not to do what I have done!* she cries out, *Spend your lives in sin and misery, in the House of the Rising Sun!* She hears Hector's steps, him coming out and standing in front of her, but she can't stop now and keeps on singing, screaming, roaring the parting shot of the last verse: *I'm going back to New Orleans, to wear that ball and chain!* She falls silent. Looks up at Hector. He actually looks terrified, bug-eyed, mouth ajar. So she has succeeded in scaring him with her song. She feels the laughter rise again and laughs so hard she chokes, can't stop, his face is priceless, imagine that, she actually managed to scare him, her jailer. Hector goes back inside, fetches a fresh bottle of poisoned water. She drinks, coughing between fits of laughter, and soon drops into that soft, hot darkness.

THE NEXT DAY Ben and Jennifer arrive. At first, when she sees their car pulling into the driveway, she feels a surge of joy, but then she looks around and realizes that the shit bucket hasn't been emptied and she's lying on the ground, like an animal, like a pig in its own filth. She is so tired and dizzy. Hasn't been able to get up and go into the house even during the hottest hours of the day. She runs her tongue over her lips. They feel chapped, scorched. Her face is burning from all the sun exposure. She feels ashamed that Ben is going see her like this. She knows this is all his fault, and yet she feels ashamed that she can be reduced to this.

Once she made love to that man in Florence, she thinks when she sees him. When she was a free person, when she was still blessed, when she was unaware that she was living in heaven.

"Ben," she whispers, "do you remember Florence?"

But Ben doesn't seem to hear her. He's standing there, looking at her with dismay. Jennifer keeps her distance and looks equally dismayed.

"We have to let her go," Ben says. "Can't you see, Jen? We have to take her back to our place, let her rest, and feed her. She can't travel like this. As soon as she's better, she'll go back home. What has he been giving her?"

Jennifer says something that sounds like the name of a pharmaceutical, a drug everyone knows about, but that she's never heard of.

"Has he really been dosing her right?" Ben wonders.

But Jennifer doesn't hear him because she's busy talking to Hector. She seems a little upset, as if she's reproaching him for something. Ben keeps staring at her. She feels giddy with laughter again. There's nothing funny about the situation, and the giddiness is probably due to Hector not knowing how to dose her, maybe he pours in a whole little bottle of the drug sometimes, and as a result upset feelings can't be summoned, the drug makes *everything* feel good. La dottoressa would have been so pleased with her. She's just sitting there peacefully, wondering: What next? No barbs as far as the eye can see. She's not swimming with her barbs out. Barbs. She waits for the word to appear in her other languages. Barbs. She waits. She should at least be able to think of it in Italian, since la dottoressa used the word not long ago. But nothing comes to her. At once, she feels her anxiety rising. Why can't her brain come up with the other words for "barbs"?

"Ben," she says, "can you get out your cell phone and google a Swedish word that I need translated into Spanish, Italian, and English?"

"What?" Ben says.

"A word. Just take out your phone and type *hullingar*. But that's in Swedish, okay? It might sound a little strange to you."

The sun is broiling. The Mississippi stinks and Noma is carrying on behind her fence. She tries to spell in English.

"*H-U-L-L-I-N-G-A-R.*"

The effort is colossal and she doesn't know if she got it right, if she in fact said the letters correctly in English. But it doesn't matter because Ben hasn't even taken out his phone, he's standing there, staring at her.

"Your phone, Ben. Please. For the sake of the Florence fucks, if nothing else. *The Florence fucks.*"

"Minnie. You're not well."

"You're not the first to say so. Il pulito said the same thing. *Minnie, you're not well, non stai bene.* But that's because you're all hell-bent on ending me! All of you. You and Il pulito! You were supposed to save me, but you're actually no better than he is. I'm closer to death now than I ever was with him. That's why I don't feel well. But fuck all that. I'm not a bitter old bitch like your Jennifer says. I don't fixate on the past, in fact I'm always looking forward. So I would be much obliged if you could take out your phone and google *hullingar.*"

But he just stands there shaking his head.

"Jen," he says slowly, "I think we have a problem here."

Jennifer comes over. Stands there awhile, looking at her.

"Sunstroke?" she says.

"No," says Ben. "This is different."

They keep looking at her.

"Can't we just kill her?" Jennifer finally says. "I mean, who cares? Shoot her in the head, or strangle her. No one knows she's here."

"Jennifer," she says. "Can you do me a favor? You all can shoot me later, but do this first. My last wish. You can give me that, even in this sadistic country, can't you? And you said the police were *sick fuckers*, but what about you and Ben? Look at me. I'm shitting in a bucket and drinking contaminated water. So could you just take out your phone and google a word for me?"

"She's gone mad," Ben says. "She's lost it."

"All the more reason," Jennifer says.

"Or maybe it is sunstroke," Ben says, "now that you mention it."

"Maybe you've broken her."

"This was your idea, Jen. We have to bring her home. I'm not in love with her or anything, but I can't see her like this."

"She's your whore, Ben. That's what you said. A sick whore from Europe. And now you want to *help* her?"

"Did you say I was a sick whore from Europe?" she says with a laugh. "That's exactly what I used to say to Mickey. I used to bring up all of his diseased whores, and now I see that Jennifer is doing the same to you . . ."

She falls serious, forgets about the barbs for a moment. Something strange is going on. There's something odd about the situation. The situation itself is, of course, bizarre, absurd, insane, she doesn't even know if it's real or if she is in fact dreaming, if she's about to be granted reprieve and wake up in bed next to Il pulito, she doesn't know, but she does know that Jennifer accusing Ben of the same thing of which she accused Il pulito is twisted in a new way, except that *she's* the diseased whore now. Some kind of vicious circle is in play. But it's hard to pinpoint how exactly. Had she been more focused and less dizzy, she might have been able to intuit her way to an answer. But now she's simply lost. It's like being in a movie that is itself a maze, an impossible figure. You enter, you walk around and see the same things from various angles but there's no way out.

"Definitely crazy," says Ben.

"*Hullingar*," she says.

Hector comes out.

"It's ready," he says. "We can bring her in now."

"What's ready?" Ben says.

"The cage," Jennifer says.

"The cage? What fucking cage?"

"The one Hector kept Rick in."

Ben takes a long look at Jennifer, then seems to enter into a minor state of panic. He's talking, no, he's screaming at Jennifer and Hector. She can't stand listening to them anymore, doesn't have it in her to collect their scattered words and try to piece them together so she can understand what's in store. After all, she's no longer the one in charge. The steamer is moving full speed ahead in an archipelago of icebergs and islets and she doesn't know who's at the helm, only that it's not her. Though doesn't she know full well who is at the helm? That's why she can't find the words for barbs, because the demon is in charge and the demon doesn't know her languages, the demon only knows its own language. A monoglot devil at the helm. All it does is sail, speeding the steamship through the night, her inner night. As Hector and Ben argue, Jennifer continues to look at her inquisitively. She holds Jennifer's gaze. She's half reclined, one foot propped on the ground, the other leg extended. She lets her knee drop to one side on the gravel, baring her genitals for Jennifer. More than that, she's smirking as she does, as if it were a challenge, a duel, a gauntlet she's throwing down for Jennifer. Jennifer is staring. Does she have any panties on? Yes, she's wearing panties. The same ones she had on when she got here, she realizes, the same ones she put on after showering and dabbing on perfume ahead of Ben's friends arriving for the surprise party. A pair of cream-white shorties with lace. The kind that Ben likes, but not Mickey. Mickey doesn't give a damn about underwear. They're coming off anyway, he'd say. Ben, on the other hand, appreciated every little thing. For this she is grateful, despite all that has happened, for this she is grateful, because she has a thing for underwear herself, considers them part of the ritual. The barbs, the damned barbs, why can't she find the words? Stop. Focus on the panties. How long has she been wearing them? One week? Two weeks? Five days? At least five days of shitting in a bucket and pissing on the ground? It goes without saying, they can't be clean. The thought fills her with laughter and she pulls up her dress as well, exposing everything: thighs, stomach, her stained panties. The last thing she sees before she glides into the fog is Jennifer bending over her, and then shouting something at Ben and Hector.

HOW LONG HAS she been asleep? She doesn't know, but she opens her eyes as she is being lifted up. Hands on her body, more hands on her body, hands grabbing hold and moving her, and all of them feel alien except two. Ben's hands. He's holding her at the waist and despite the situation, despite the fact that she is being carried by strangers who could drop her at any moment or might simply let go, she feels his warmth and in turn is warmed. The presence of another human being, touch. This is what her body is responding to. This is the beauty of the flesh—perhaps its only beauty—the capacity to respond in a tender and dignified way to the presence of another human being's flesh. She wonders if she is able to feel Ben's warmth this clearly because she is close to death? If the body, when that is what one is, allows its longing one last bloom, like a sudden flowering in the savanna?

When she wakes up again, she is indeed in a cage. She sees them standing in a row on the other side of the bars, all three of them. Unmoving, they watch her. Jennifer with disgust in her eyes, Ben with concern, Hector neutral, as if he were assessing the strength of the bars rather than looking at her. Her throat burns.

"Can I have something to drink, please? I'm thirsty."

Ben holds out a water bottle.

"Poisoned or pure?" she says.

"Pure," he says.

She understands. So she hasn't been given a sedative. The difference is undeniable. Now everything feels frightening in a way it didn't when they were still out in the sun. She is sitting in a cage at the long end of Hector's shack. The cage is tall and wide enough for her to squat in or lie down flat. The bars are not particularly narrow set, but too close together for her to squeeze through.

"You've got to get me out of here, Ben," she says and starts to cry.

Ben sits down by the bars.

"Minnie, listen to me. I will get you out of here. I'll get you out, but you've got to give me a little time."

"How much time?" she says, tears streaming down her cheeks.

"A few days, I'll be back in a few days."

Ben stays there for a while with his hand through the bars, stroking her hair with compassion. Jennifer paces irritably around them. Finally she kicks Ben in the leg and tosses her head to indicate that they should hit the road. From the cage, she watches Ben walk off; he doesn't turn around.

After they leave, Hector takes a seat out on the porch with a book. She asks what he's reading. He doesn't answer. She hears the riverboat blowing its horn. He fetches another bottle of cloudy water. She gulps it down. So this is what this existence demands of me, she thinks, so this is what I must endure right now. Actually, it's no surprise. I was in a cage in Florence too. That was a cage with invisible bars, a cage I could have left much sooner had I come to my senses and kept a cool head. But since I was unable to come to my senses and keep a cool head through it all, reality had to make my confinement concrete. That is why I am now concretely in an iron cage. I am trying to draw some sort of lesson from this, but am beginning to suspect that it is too late.

In the evening, the heat sets in again. It rises from the damp ground like a stifling amber fever only to hover above the flat landscape. Gone is all possibility of escape. She is caught in this stagnant lowland. Perhaps she will never see Il pulito again. Perhaps she will never again feel his hands on her body, inhale his scent in the darkness, sleep beside the wild beast at night.

She wakes at midnight. Hector is sitting on a chair with his back to her. At first she lies there in silence, trying to determine whether or not Hector is asleep. He is not. He scratches his thigh with one hand, checks his cell phone. Then all is still and quiet again. She says, quickly and in a clear voice, "I'm awake."

Hector flinches, turns around, and looks at her in horror. So she scared him. Well, good. She may be benefiting from a helping hand now, but it's still commendable that she managed to accept said help. In silence she drills her gaze into his back. She knows he can sense it, but it's as if he doesn't want to turn around, as if he doesn't want to confirm that she is in fact sitting there in the room, peering at him through the darkness.

IT STARTS RAINING a few hours later, just before dawn. Hard and dogged, the storm moves in, as if announcing an imminent apocalypse. She hears pounding on the roof and the ominous creaks in the windbeaten walls. It's not like the wind in Europe, this Caribbean wind, a blind and rowdy wind, a wind that rushes forth, wild and speeding. Normally she would have been terrified, but not now. Now she is calm and can do what she should: Lie perfectly still and wait for the demon to further materialize, for it to take the helm. There she lies. Breathing, trying to unleash the power from the darkness inside her. Far away are the words. Far away are the barbs. Far away are the paranoid multilingual recitations. The demon speaks only its own language. The demon is silent.

"I'm here," she whispers, "I'm here, but you can take the wheel."

She waits. The rain and the wind pound harder and harder.

"Can you hear me? If you want to see the other demon again, you must take the wheel now."

All of a sudden she notices something. Hector has left his chair and is sitting on the floor with his back against the wall, not far from the cage. He is asleep. On his belt hangs the key chain, and on the key chain hangs the key to her cage. It's right there, plain and clear, the key chain, along with what she assumes is the key to her cage. It's strange that an object so small and trivial-seeming can mean so very much to her. The chain looks to be out of reach, but since she can now count on the demon's help, perhaps she should try anyway. She presses herself against the bars. Pushes one leg out. Her foot slips right through, the ankle and calf no problem, it's the knee that gets stuck. She has to push hard and it feels like the internal structure of the joint is being dislocated, but she gets it through. She has lost so much weight over the past few days that her whole thigh slides through as well. When she feels the steel rod against her groin, despite the absurdity of the situation, a rush runs through her. The steel against her groin reminds her of Il pulito. His body, him gripping her. She laughs to herself. Imagine if she started masturbating. Grinding herself against the iron bar, in this shack, in this swamp, in this foreign city, with the rain on the roof and the storm in the walls, with her sleeping jailer and most of her body in the cage, only her leg outside. If she achieved orgasm like this, then it would really say something about her. She pictures herself telling Il pulito this story. About how, when reaching for the keys to the cage, she felt the iron between her legs and came to think of him and so, before she plucked the keys from the jailer's belt with her toes, she'd actually masturbated, actually had an orgasm against that cold, hard bar. Il pulito would have laughed, saying, *Cazzo Minnie, you're incredible, I can't believe you did that, it says something*

about you, about us. She laughs. But then it's as if the demon taps
her on the shoulder to say, "Hey there. The key. You're supposed
to be taking the key." She wants to cry. She's so far gone that,
by comparison, the demon appears to be the picture of reason.
She is in the thick of misery. The misery of flesh, the misery of
bodily fluids. The pleasing metal between her legs, pressing into
her groin and between her buttocks. How could she be feeling
this, this arousal, after all that arousal has cost her? She is, as
they said in her village, "priceless." True, she only bears partial
responsibility because the demon also has a hand in the game,
but still, what a devilish grip she finds herself caught in, what a
devilish grip she has *allowed* herself to be caught in. Cursed lust.
This cursed lust that has laid waste to so much of her life. This
cursed flesh planted there, smug and unwavering at the controls, driving. But she has to stop thinking about it now. She has
to stop thinking these draining thoughts, because if she turns
too far away from her dark side, the demon might weaken, and
then she won't accomplish anything, then she will sit here, die,
rot in this cage. So keep cool. After the demon has helped her,
she will outsmart it. She knows how, she's an adroit manipulator. She has learned from a great master, she has been listening
and learning for so long that she has finally understood how
to manipulate the master himself. That's basic survival. Listen
and learn, swim through the mesh of a net, bypass every other
creature's barbs, even those of demons. But now: laser focus
on Hector's keys. She reaches her foot out. She presses into the
metal rod so hard her whole pelvis aches. But she has to press a
little harder. It feels like her dirty panties are being wedged into
her vagina. What if she hurts herself so badly that she wrecks
her genitals? Yes, and? Would that really be a tragedy, wouldn't

it rather be the solution to all the misery she has brought upon herself? If her genitals hadn't always held sway, she could have been thinking rationally from the start. If her genitals had not been holding the compass, she would never have stayed with Il pulito longer than a day at most. So let them be wrecked, she thinks, as long as I can urinate, I'll be fine, now I'm taking that key. Her toes have reached Hector. A little more pressure. She can do it. She clings to the rod in front of her to get the leverage to push down a little harder. Finally, she achieves the unlikely. Even though her toes feel too short, too stubby, even though they have none of the mobility of fingers, even though they are so clumsy and unfit, she succeeds. As if the demon were standing by Hector's side and helping her slip Hector's key chain down over her little toe without friction. She feels a giggle percolating, so intense it makes her tear up. She feels like giving in to a maniacal, hysterical fit of laughter, but she controls herself, pushes the laughter back, and grips the key chain for all she's worth, pulls her foot back and brings it into the cage. She has to jerk her knee, a quick hard jerk that feels like it's jeopardizing her knee joint, but the pieces inside seem to slide back into place and now the key chain is inside the cage. She sits there in total silence, looking at Hector. He appears to be fast asleep. It's the heat and the sound of the rain on the roof that brings about such a deep sleep. Warmth and wetness, it's like a return to the womb.

She fumbles with the keys. There's really only one that could fit the padlock and she quickly identifies it. Even with her heart pounding in her temples, she manages to unlock it. It's because the demon is helping her. She's just going with it. Letting herself be led. The demon will assist in her every endeavor. That's it. Unhook the lock, open the cage. Crawl out, give your muscles a quick stretch. Stand up and find your balance. Tiptoe across the floor. After sitting still for so long you wobble, but you do walk, you make your way, that's all that matters. Open the door and go out into the rain. It's muddy, so your feet slip and slide in the mud, but you make your way. One foot in front of the other. All the way down the driveway, slipping and landing on your tailbone in the mud but your groin is as good as ruined anyway so what's a few more bruises, on your feet again, onto Noma's property, everything will be fine because something else is driving, something else wants to keep moving forward, just go with it, a comforting iron hand holding you upright, protecting you from the light and giving you everything you need as long as you stay in the shadows, it's furnishing you with every thought and impulse needed to bring about the reunion. The reunion of the demons. Noma's door is unlocked and swings open, slowly and silently. She lingers in the doorway. Looks into Noma's living room. The night radio is speaking to the blind. From the doorway, she sees Noma sitting there, at the table, as if awaiting her. She clears her throat. It's exactly as she wanted it to be, it's like a helpful dream, and yet these are the only words she finds: "You're up late."

The woman's glassy gaze seems to be on her. Noma nods amiably, then drinks from a cup and reaches for what appears to be a platter of pink cookies.

"I'm always up this late," she says, taking a bite of cookie. Then she turns her gaze to the ceiling. "It's raining, but the roof seems to be holding tight. That's good, it means it'll be a little while yet before the apocalypse gets here."

She lingers in the doorway, awaiting instructions from the demon. Hello? What should she do now?

"So you've arrived?" Noma says, as if to help her along.

She slowly makes her way to the table, pulls out a chair, and sits down across from Noma.

"Yes," she says. "I've arrived."

Noma nods. Pink crumbs cling to her mouth and her eyes are bright, shining.

"Tell me something about yourself," Noma says.

"About myself?" she says.

"About you, and your childhood."

The situation is still absurd, but in a different way than it was a few minutes ago. Everything is moving very fast now, but she mustn't stop to think, she just has to go with it, let the situation drive.

"My childhood, you say. My childhood." She clears her throat and continues: "Well, for some years I lived a few miles from a great demon. And I sometimes wonder what effect it had on me. Maybe you could tell me? Could the demon, who lived a few miles away, have altered me in some way?"

Noma nods gravely, as if her words are of the utmost importance.

"It has affected you," she says. "To the greatest extent. One can see it on you. It has left a mark, long scratches that glow in the dark."

"Are you saying that you can *see* them?"

Noma folds her hands.

"Can I see them? They're shining so brightly I have to squint, those scratch marks inside you, they're blinding!"

She clears her throat again. When she realizes the depth of understanding with which she is being met, it frightens her. Her throat seems to swell shut, as if from a surge of emotion, because this kind of understanding is new to her: being taken seriously, and respected, especially after having bared the unvarnished extent of her inner confusion. Is such understanding possible? No, of course not. It's all so alien, and yet she feels as if, after a long trek through the labyrinth, she has finally come to a place that feels familiar, a place where she can rest and perhaps even find a way out.

"Do you have a telephone, Noma?"

"Who are you going to call?"

"Il pulito. Mickey."

"The one who's going to show up in a car and save you?"

"Yes, exactly. The one who's going to save me. But we don't have much time, Noma, so if you do have a phone, could you maybe get it out now?"

"I have a phone."

"And?"

"Are you sure about this?"

"Absolutely."

"Why?"

"Because I love him so much it feels like I'm going to break."

"It happens," says Noma.

"How?"

"Some people cut off a connection, a relationship, maybe even a marriage, because they think it's no good, that it's destroying them."

Her voice is hoarse, almost a whisper, when she speaks, as if she had feeble, defective vocal cords that are now being strained to their limit.

"But they're wrong," she continues. "Because when they do get out into the world, they end up in something even worse. An even worse situation, a far more devastating destruction."

"That's exactly how it went for me," she says, nodding, "exactly like that."

"I know," says Noma. "So now all I need is to hear how much you love him and how much you've suffered. If you're convincing, I'll give you the phone."

"There are no words," she says, shaking her head.

"There are always words, *my child*, you just have to find them."

My child? What a lovely turn of phrase. What if she could have been Noma's *child*. Then, despite the shack, despite Noma's blindness and advanced age, she would have felt safe. What a force, what a woman, *caring* for you. She closes her eyes. She mustn't get sentimental, she mustn't lose focus. She can't pressure Noma. Everything takes its time. Her groin aches. She remembers Il pulito, she remembers Florence. She starts to cry.

"How I loved him, Noma. You can't imagine. We eventually found ourselves in a kind of edgeland, it's true, but I loved it all, all his flesh, all his manly vileness, I loved it all. If a woman can be born to love, that birth was mine and that woman was me. I'm telling you. The two of you. You and the demon. No woman has ever loved like Minnie loved Mickey. No one has ever allowed herself be torn apart like I have, no one has ever surrendered to such an extent. There may be women more beautiful, more elegant, more eloquent, more pleasing than I am, but when it comes to the flesh, Noma, demon, when it comes to the flesh they all pale in comparison. When it comes to the flesh, I am the one who knows the most about the magnitude of suffering."

Noma nods in satisfaction. "That's the spirit." She opens a box on the table. "Here you go. Here's the telephone."

She takes the phone out of the box slowly and as if captivated. A very real phone. An iPhone, its battery charged and with coverage, five whole bars.

"Make your call. Call your savior."

She dials Il pulito. Numbers, prefixes, and all, she doesn't slip up once. He answers after two rings.

"Mickey?"

"Minnie?"

"Listen to me. I don't have much time. Just listen."

She says that she's in trouble, she's in New Orleans and she's been kidnapped and he's got to come help her. Il pulito seems to understand the gravity of the situation, because he simply asks for her exact coordinates. She breathes a sigh of relief. It's the bodyguard in him. He knows what information is required in any operation, he doesn't get caught up in emotion, he gathers the facts as fast as he can, then takes the necessary measures. She opens the cell phone's GPS, takes a screenshot and sends him the coordinates. It all proceeds without a hitch. The image travels across the marshes, the swamps, the ocean, the Alps, and reaches Il pulito's cell phone in Florence.

"I'll be right there, Minnie," he says. "I'll see who can come with me, and I'll go right to the airport. All you have to do is survive another day. If you escaped from the place where they were holding you to make this call, go back to that place now, make sure your kidnappers don't get suspicious, or they'll kill you and dispose of your body before I get there. Go do that now. We'll see each other soon."

She is crying with relief as she hands the phone back to Noma. Noma reaches out and strokes her cheek.

"Can you hear that?" she says. "The wind has died down."

She is immediately aware of the oppressive silence that now surrounds the shack. Then she turns, walks through Noma's living room, across Noma's property, back to Hector, who's still asleep by the cage, his rifle propped against the wall behind him. She attaches the key to his belt loop, crawls into the cage and closes the padlock. Right before she falls asleep, through the half-open front door she sees the first light of dawn slowly spreading across the sky.

FOR THE NEXT seventy-two hours she is a model prisoner. She sits nicely in her cage, shits obediently in the bucket, doesn't complain when the cockroaches scurry across her legs or when Hector forgets to give her the can of white beans in tomato sauce at lunchtime. She even takes up humming and starts asking Hector personal questions. How long has he lived in New Orleans, what does he think of America's gun laws, does he know anything about Florence, and what does he think of her as a person, does he think they would have talked to each other if they met at a party? Hector makes his usual hand gesture and says he'd really appreciate it if she'd shut her trap. But he says it in a different way, and she can sense that she has thawed him out a bit after all, because he's walking with a lighter step, looking at her more often, and even humming a tune though he stops dead if she starts humming along. He also calls Jennifer to say that he doesn't know if she's gone completely insane or completely sane, but maybe they should reassess because the marks on her face are gone at least. She tenses up when she hears this. It would not be good if Ben and Jennifer showed up at the wrong moment.

When Il pulito comes to rescue her, Hector has to be the only one here, because Il pulito can handle Hector, Hector is small and frail, like a skin-encrusted chicken drumstick on legs, but Hector plus Ben and Jennifer might overpower him. Besides, she doesn't want anything to happen to Ben. He may not have managed to save her like she wished he would, but he's still Ben, and she wouldn't be able to forgive herself if Il pulito hurt him. Or if he hurt Il pulito, for that matter. It's all so mixed up. It's the heat, the water, and the demon. Anyway, Hector seems to have arranged for Jennifer and Ben to come the day after tomorrow. She sits in the cage and makes an effort to smile big once he's off the phone.

"Are you going to let me go?" she says. "Hooray!"

"We've gotta do something," Hector says. "I have a life to get back to, I get paid next to nothing to sit here watching you."

"I'm insulted," she says with a wink. "You should get paid much more to watch a person like me."

"We'll either have to let you go or kill you," Hector says.

"You're just putting that out there?" she says. "How do you think it makes me feel when you say that you might kill me?" She says this theatrically, not sure how she's managing to keep the fear at bay, but she is.

"I don't know how you feel," Hector says with a cold little laugh. "And it's not my concern either."

"Can I have some more water, please? And white beans if you have them. I don't understand how a city could have been built here, in the middle of this swamp and heat."

"New Orleans is a nice city. A nice, colorful city."

"Certainly. I would have loved to stroll through the French Quarter, sit in a secret vampire bar, or, why not, go on an alligator safari in the bayou. But I didn't get to do any of that! I've only had a worm's-eye view of this city, Hector. Wriggling around in the dirt, that's all I've gotten to do. Don't ask me to take a liking to New Orleans. Or you, for that matter."

Hector gives her a long inscrutable look. Finally, he cracks a smile. "Do you want something to eat?" he says. "You must be tired of beans."

"I wouldn't say no."

"I could go out for a po'boy."

"What if I run away while you're gone?"

"You couldn't."

"Maybe I have powers."

"You don't have powers," Hector says with a laugh. "If you had powers, you'd have gotten out a long time ago."

"Sure, so you say. All right then. How about that po'boy?"

He gives her a dubious look. She knows he's thinking through all the risks of leaving her alone for a while. But she also knows that he feels compelled to go buy that po'boy, not so much for her as for himself. She sees the way he's looking at Noma's house, how he's assessing the woman as a risk factor. She closes her eyes and falls asleep. When she wakes up, it's evening. Hector is nowhere to be seen, and the night radio for the blind is playing in Noma's house. Outside the cage is a po'boy wrapped in paper. She takes it as a sign of respect, respect that, along with the nourishment from the sausage, bread, and sauce, gives her the energy to summon a little more strength.

FROM TIME TO time she wakes up and thinks that the telephone conversation with Il pulito was part of a delirium. A side effect of the drug and the heat, a nocturnal hallucination in captivity. She's probably going to die here. In all likelihood she will die here, but she figures the prison guards will feel sorry enough for her so as not to make her suffer. If Ben and Jennifer turn up and decide to kill her, Ben will make sure it's quick and painless. They won't suffocate her. She doesn't want to be suffocated. If she had a choice, she'd want to die of a morphine overdose. That can't go wrong, can it? As she's thinking these thoughts she realizes that she doesn't know the word for "barbs" in any language but Swedish anymore, and this fact suggests that all is not as it should be, in a way that bodes well for this situation.

The sun rises and sets. As it sets, it lingers a while on the horizon like a malevolent fiery eye, only to then be swallowed by the sea.

THE DAY IL PULITO arrives in New Orleans begins like any other. She doesn't know how many days have passed, if Ben and Jennifer have arrived, all she knows is that she is not dead, she is still alive and in the cage. Hector brings water, calls Jennifer, empties the shit bucket—all the while she's talking to him. *How are you today, Hector, isn't it even hotter today, can't I get out of the cage, when is Ben coming, when is Ben coming, when is Ben coming?* Finally he says he can't deal with her anymore and he's going to go into the city for a while.

"It went well last time," she says, "so you don't have to worry."

Hector leaves. His car disappears across the burnt earth. He has left the door open so she can see outside. She sits in the cage, looking out the door. She lies down, curls up in the fetal position. After a while, she sees another car come by. It drives slowly, stops several times on the main road, turns around, and finally pulls into the driveway leading up to the house. It's a black BMW. It's Il pulito. She knows it's him, it's exactly the kind of car he would rent if he had to rent a car abroad. The car stops outside the shack and the engine shuts off. For one brief moment total silence reigns. Then the car doors open and they get out. It's Il pulito and two of his friends, Michele and Dino. She has seen them in pictures, Michele is a policeman in Naples, Dino is military and stationed at one of the NATO bases on the Adriatic. They stand there, surveying the area. Her heart throbs as she watches Il pulito walk around. Tears well in her eyes and she tries to call out for help, but none of them hear her because her voice is weak and once again there is a hot driving wind. Finally they walk up to the shack and the open door. Dino is the first to lay eyes on her.

"What the hell," he says and draws his weapon.

Il pulito and Michele follow behind him with their weapons drawn. They secure the premises, checking behind all the doors and in the bedroom and toilet. They establish that no one else is in the building, and then the three of them end up standing by the cage, staring at her dumbly. She stares back. She notices that Il pulito has gotten thin. He looks taller, gangly almost. And older, he looks older. He has aged in these weeks, they've worn on him too. Nothing compared to her, that goes without saying, but he too has suffered and this is proof of his love. She takes all this in, registers it, until it dawns on her how she must look to them.

"Christ, what a stink," seems to be all Il pulito can get out.

They take some tools from the trunk of the car and in a few minutes they've got the padlock open. They give her a sports drink and a package of cookies that Dino takes out of a bag. She wants them to leave right away, before Hector gets back, but they don't want to, they say that they're here to have their fun too.

"And what fun is that?" she asks.

"Is the man you betrayed me with the one who's holding you captive?" Il pulito says.

She nods.

"Then we have things to do before we clear out," he says.

"What things?"

He looks at her with surprise. "We're going to kill the bastard, of course."

She says it's not his fault, and Il pulito tells her that he knows, but it's been a while since he's killed anyone and he thinks the bastard she's been screwing around with would fit the ticket pretty damn well. He'll splatter these walls with his brains. He wipes the sweat from his brow.

"What about me?" she says.

"I'll deal with you in time."

"You didn't come all this way just to beat me to death?" she says with a wry smile.

No, he hasn't, but her actions will have consequences. Yes, sure, she says, she knows, but they'll have to save that for later, they really should be getting out of here.

Michele parks the car behind the shack. Then the four of them sit down, backs to the living room walls, and wait. She sits between Il pulito and Dino. She looks at Il pulito's powerful arm, the dark hair covering his tanned skin. She listens to his breathing, which is as calm as can be. She wonders if they'll actually buy that she had a relationship with Hector. A dried-up old man in a shack. But they don't ask any questions and she gets the sense that they don't want to know, all they want is an outlet and almost any living creature will do. They sit like that for a long time before Hector finally comes back. He trundles up to the house, parks by the stoop, and gets out of the car. He stops in his tracks as soon as he notices that the cage is open. Then he climbs the stairs with a few quick strides. His old, wizened body practically flies up the steps, and then he stands there in the doorway looking for her with a wild, burning gaze, and when he realizes that she is not alone but sitting alongside three armed men, he tries to make his escape. But Dino is after him like an arrow, floors him, grabs his neck, and guides him back into the living room. They tape his mouth shut and tie him to a chair.

"You're telling me that you screwed this old man?" Il pulito says.

"It's what's inside that counts," she says.

He laughs out loud. "You're lying, Minnie. You're lying."

She doesn't answer.

"I was looking forward to someone more full of life," he says, "this guy's got one foot in the grave."

"Can't you just let him go?" she says. "Can't we just leave?"

Il pulito pays her no mind and starts unbuttoning his shirt cuffs.

"Now let's have our fun, man-to-man," he says, rolling up his sleeves. "Go wait in the car, Minnie. Cover your ears if you don't want to listen."

Half an hour later they emerge. They are silent, but she senses satisfaction in the air, as if they have undergone some kind of shared catharsis.

"What did you do?" she asks. "Did you torture him?"

"You don't want to know," Il pulito says. "But I can tell you that his last wish was that he'd never laid eyes on you."

She turns and watches the shack fall out of view. The last thing she sees through the rear window is Noma standing on her property, watching them go. She's holding her hands out in front of her, fingers raised in a cross.

THE FLIGHT TAKES almost a full day and during that day she tries to chat, lighten the mood, talk about New Orleans. Michele and Dino barely speak to her, Il pulito talks to her but there is an underlying chill in his voice, a chill that makes her stomach clench with fresh dread. It is now that she must prove herself capable. The demon has helped her get this far. Now she must outwit the demon.

"When can we talk?" she whispers to him during their layover in London.

"We'll talk when we get home," Il pulito says. "In peace and quiet, when we get home."

"I'm sorry," she whispers. "I want you to forgive me for what I've done."

Il pulito doesn't appear to have heard her.

"I'm sorry," she whispers again. "I'll do whatever you want. Whatever you want if you forgive me."

"Okay, then shut your mouth," he says.

She understands. Sometimes you have to leave people be. Sit in silence. Aware of your crime and completely silent. She has to steel herself for what this way comes but babbling on and making pathetic pleas don't help a thing. *Can't bullshit a bullshitter*, sit still and shut your mouth. The plane flies in over the Dolomites, on over the Apennines, and finally they land in Florence. They say goodbye to Dino and Michele at the airport, their respective connecting flights are in a few hours.

"Thank you for saving me," she says, but they don't meet her gaze, they hug Il pulito and look at him with what she can't interpret as anything but a mixture of pity and happiness.

They go to the parking lot. There's the car. It must be more than a hundred degrees inside it. She wonders how long her trial will take when they get back home, if she can shower beforehand, and what they're having for dinner. They walk into the apartment and the familiar smell of them hits her. Home, she thinks. The farther away you've been, the wilder waters you've sailed, the homier and safer home feels. Il pulito has sparkling water and cold white wine in the fridge. She takes a long, cool shower, puts on clean clothes and throws the old ones in the trash. She spends a long time looking at her dirty panties on top of coffee grounds. She wonders who found Hector's body. Noma? Ben?

"As you know, you can't do something like this to me with impunity," Il pulito says when they're sitting at the table.

She knows. She says as much: "I absolutely do know. Everything has just gone so incredibly wrong."

But there is one thing she's sure of now, and it's that there is a demon living inside her doing things to a demon that's living inside him. If only they could exorcise these demons, then they'd probably be able to have a good relationship. In time. If they manage to exorcise the demons and go back to la dottoressa. Then everything could be fine. They will learn to love each other in a more adult and responsible way. She's been held captive for so long and has had time to think, so she's figured a few things out.

"*Ma che cazzo dici?*" he says, What the hell are you saying?

He says that there's one thing she has to understand, and that's from here on out she has to stop talking so much shit. He wouldn't have thought twice about killing her that instant, if it weren't for the fact that he loves her and has shared so much with her and that if she were to disappear from his life it would leave too big a void, a void he could never fill. So it's purely egotistical. Had he not been standing in his own way, he'd have killed her on the spot. Despite the darkness in his eyes, she takes it as a joke.

"Exactly," she says, "that's how it is for me too. I would have killed you too if I wasn't standing in my own way." She laughs. It's the wine, and the relief.

"Minnie. Can you keep your mouth shut when I'm talking? Because this isn't going to be fun, Minnie, no fun at all, for you. I have to figure out a way to be sure that you're mine and can't hurt me. So the *whore* in you can't go out and hurt me. There will be no fun in it for you. It won't be much fun for me either, but even less for you. You might as well be aware of that now, so you don't go out and get any ideas about what's coming to you."

His eyes are hard and ice-cold as he speaks.

"What do you mean?" she says, feeling the now-familiar dread return.

"I don't know what I mean yet. But I do have to figure it out. It will take the time it takes, and in that time I want you to do everything in your power not to upset me."

She promises. They make love. He is gentle and tender. Afterward, she can't hold back her tears. She cries and her nose runs on his shoulder and he lies perfectly still, looking into the darkness as he slowly strokes her face.

SHE WALKS THROUGH Florence. She tries to channel the feeling she had before she left for New Orleans, but it's as if the images are superimposed on each other and she can't keep the cities apart. It's as if the moisture from the facades and the clouds of insects above the Arno are remnants of the marsh-land around Hector's shack, remnants that are now a part of her and thus have come back with her, a photopic receipt of her inexorable change. She sees herself reflected in the shop-windows and notes that she is unbecomingly skinny. Angular and malnourished. She looks sick. She wonders if she looks like his sister when she was sick. She thinks Il pulito must be disappointed. To have traveled that far only to bring home a woman this hideous. It's possible that he thinks it might not have been worth the effort.

But why does everything have to be so hard? Can't she just try to see things in a different light? Isn't there birdsong in the air? Isn't a cool, considered rain falling on her face? Isn't it a wonderful time of year, and isn't Florence a city in a class of its own? She walks past a small basement restaurant, orders dumplings, which she eats out of a foil container with chopsticks as the rain pools on the cobbles outside. When she has finished eating, she sits, sated, looking up at the buildings around her. How does this city maintain its facade of sheer, feminine beauty throughout the centuries? She thinks of the marsh and the lowland. The marsh and the lowland were a better reflection of her, there was harmony between interior and exterior. She thinks of Hector again. She wonders how he died. She thinks of Ben. She feels bruised inside when she thinks of Ben. The opportunity she had with him, of having a good life, if she had only kept a cool head. Everything aches. Il pulito aches, Ben aches, Florence aches, and New Orleans aches. It's as if the very air around her has begun to ache. She looks up at the sky. One fine day she will die, she thinks, and then at least there will be an end to all her pain.

She gets up and walks on. Again she notes that she does not feel well. She is sick and needs help, but she won't get any. She is sick and must heal herself, there is nothing to pray for. She is simply sick and must heal herself.

AND SHE IS truly doing her best now. Self-control, calm, and the full degree of human warmth a person in her condition can muster, all to bring about a turnaround. It won't be easy, but she's stubborn. Stubbornness and focus, perhaps this very combination is her greatest strength. It's like she's swum deep into a cave and the oxygen is starting to run out. She has to stay calm so as not to consume more air than necessary as she swims back through the black, anoxic water. So all she has to do is get out. One stroke at a time, until suddenly she finds herself on the outside once more, in the fresh air where the water is bright, clear, and kind. In the meantime, she has to stay in control of whatever comes her way. Sacred edifices are good, they still have an effect, when you are close to them the demons lose their power. When they go for a walk in the evenings, she makes sure they walk past churches, suggesting they sit with their backs pressed to the old stone walls. As they sit, she can feel the demons' power diminishing, the kindness and understanding between them growing. The day will come when she will need to banish her demon once and for all. It might be difficult, because

the demon expects something of her now. Something in return. It takes more than a snap of the fingers to outsmart
a demon. She has no idea how to go about it. She needs to
find someone who knows about these things, but how? She'd
need to discuss this with someone, but the only person she
talks to is Il pulito, and she can't share these thoughts with
him. Besides, it has to be someone in possession of the rel-
evant knowledge. An exorcist. Some sort of old priest who
is familiar with this type of phenomenon, someone who has
not taken part in modernity, someone who has stayed out of
it because he or she has borne witness and gained a deep understanding and then kept silent, because the understanding
of certain phenomena is impossible to share in these modern times. How does one go about finding an old priest, the
kind that they now need? The answer seems obvious: One
visits environs frequented by such priests. She doesn't know
offhand what those environs might be, but she decides to be
receptive to any ideas that might occur to her from now on.

This decision might be the reason why, one afternoon,
when she sees an ad on the bus for a restaurant just outside
Florence, she thinks that it might be a good place to begin
her search for an exorcist. The restaurant is located on a small
hill in a building that has been an abbey for many centuries. L'Abbazia degli Angeli Beati. It sounds very good, and
promising. The Abbey of the Blessed Angels, that should be
a good place to start. She suggests they go there. Have dinner at L'Abbazia. It's about a half-hour drive outside of Florence, high atop a mountain, which means the last stretch of
the drive is on switchback roads. She's afraid that Il pulito
will dismiss the idea, too far away and too stressful a drive on

those roads after a few glasses of wine, but after perusing the menu on the abbey's website, he nods slowly and says it will be interesting. He calls and makes a reservation. They go there the very next evening.

It is of the utmost importance, she realizes, that things be as relaxed as possible between them during the journey and their visit so that she can take in the surroundings and see what they might hold. But Il pulito has had a bad day at work, some customer overseas has filed a complaint about a batch of brakes and his phone is already hot as they traverse Florence. His driving is angry and abrupt, he's gesticulating and shouting in broken English while occasionally raising his fist and pounding the steering wheel in a rage. She tries to mouth Calm down, *ma calmati, amore, calmati,* but he doesn't look her way. Finally, she puts a hand on his thigh, which seems to be the straw that breaks the camel's back. He slaps it away while screaming *Porca puttana is it impossible for you to leave me alone? Keep your hands off me, off, off!*

She must not allow herself to feel insulted. It's his demon screaming at her demon, she sees through the game and so she calmly removes her hand, places it on her own thigh and turns to face the window. She sits like that, looking out. On the radio "Stand by Your Man" by Tammy Wynette is playing. She should be fearing for her life because Il pulito is now in fact driving like a maniac on these winding roads, but she pushes away the fear because she realizes that any action on her part will only aggravate the situation. She doesn't know if she's suppressing the fear or if what she's experiencing is something she's read about called *frozen fright,* a way for a victim to avoid triggering a perpetrator's violent instincts any more than necessary. She doesn't know if there's a difference. *Frozen fright* occurs when instinct chooses paralysis over panic. She tries not to dwell on it. Things are what they are, whatever you call them. Finally, they arrive. Il pulito parks.

"Terribly sorry, Minnie," he says after he's shut off the engine, "but I have to sort this out before I can go in. You'll have to take the table for now. My name. I'll be right there, just give me a few minutes."

She's glad he sounds . . . if not friendly, then at least not angry.

"I'll be fine," she says, and gets out of the car.

She walks up the hill toward the entrance. The abbey looms before her, a bit stark, but beautiful and imposing. Ivy hangs down some of the walls and, farther out, over the slopes upon which the monastery seems to be balancing. The view is marvelous. This is a sacred place. She can feel it, this is how they make a body feel, sacred places. When she opens the door to the restaurant, she is met with an enveloping calm. A warmth redolent of wax candles and the soft amiable murmuring of other diners. No noisy parties shouting, just hushed conversation. The contrast to their journey is overwhelming. She can't remember the last time she entered this kind of environment. It's a bit like stepping straight into heaven. She feels something in her chest opening up, as if she could breathe again and so be filled with warm cotton wool. The furnishings are simple, the tables and chairs seem to be made of untreated wood. Old faded frescoes can be seen on the thick stone walls and candles are burning in great wall-mounted candelabras. Italy, she thinks, Italy. Everything else is irrelevant.

A man comes up to her, introduces himself as Giovanni, the owner, and when she says Il pulito's name, he shows her to a round table at the far end of the restaurant.

"He'll be here soon," she says apologetically, "he just had to take a call."

Giovanni nods and smiles. "I'll bring the menu in the meantime. Something to drink?"

"A glass of water, please," she says.

Then she sits there, with the water and the menu. She has time to read it through once and then once more. She has left her cell phone in the apartment, so after having gone through the menu twice she's at a loss for what to do. She looks around. Time passes. She thinks she is on the receiving end of pitying glances from a woman at a nearby table. A woman sitting across from a man, enjoying his full attention. As it should be. Eventually the owner returns with a bottle and a glass. He resolutely places the glass in front of her and fills it.

"On the house," he says.

She can tell by his movements and the way he's looking at her that he understands the situation. Perhaps he has seen Il pulito through the window, pacing while on his call. He has understood that she is sitting here waiting for a man who does not respect her, and so he wants to offer her some form of comfort. The joy she first feels when he pours the wine slowly turns to shame. She can think of nothing sadder than a woman sitting alone drinking wine while waiting for a dinner companion who is ignoring her. At once she feels so interminably downcast—how could any part of her life have become this hopeless! She closes her eyes and tries to commune with the sacrality of the room. The demon seems calm.

She focuses on that. The demon is calm and she has come here to find an exorcist, and thanks to Il pulito's absence she can sit here searching for one.

Diagonally across from her, in fact, is a man dining alone. Every now and then he looks up at her, every now and then she looks up at him. She briefly considers whether some benevolent force has paved the way and placed the man she needs to drive out the demons right in front of her, but she quickly dismisses the thought. He is too young. Fifty at most. He can't possibly be in possession of the kind of ancient knowledge she requires. She looks away in disappointment, takes a big gulp of wine. The man keeps watching her. She looks up, meets his gaze, and thinks she sees the hint of a smile. She chuckles to herself. If only he knew. If only he knew how she had been sitting like this a few months earlier, exchanging glances with a different man, and how that gave rise to a turbulence and a meltdown from which she will probably never fully recover, then he'd have understood that she doesn't do this anymore. She no longer sits around exchanging glances with strange men, because she knows the type of catastrophe it can give rise to. She gets up and walks to the toilet. As she pees, she hears the door open and someone enters the next booth. She flushes, goes out, and washes her hands in the sink. She hears a flush come from the other toilet and then the man from the table opposite comes out. He plants himself next to her, at the neighboring sink, and washes his hands too. There they are. Soaping their hands and rinsing the lather away, they reach for the paper towels at the same time. A moment of embarrassment arises. He takes a quick step back and says with a little laugh, "You first."

She takes her paper towel and as she's wiping her hands she notices the way he's smiling at her in the mirror. She doesn't smile back. She throws the paper in the trash and goes back to her table to continue waiting for Il pulito. Soon after, the man comes out of the toilet, goes to his seat, sits down. As soon as he's in his chair, he looks at her and smiles. The situation in the toilet seems to have triggered him. Some men operate like that, they make advances to be sure that they're being rejected, because that's the kind of woman they want, someone they can trust, someone they know won't smile back, and once they've established that you're not that kind of available person, they kick it up a notch. Feeling utterly depleted, she leans back in her chair and crosses her arms over her chest and then sits there, staring blankly into space. Giovanni refills her glass. The man diagonally across from her seems to get more excited the more time passes and the more she ignores him. He eats his dessert and drinks his coffee. All the while she feels him communicating with her somehow, his hope in the air. She reluctantly acknowledges what it is that he's imagining. Two lonely souls brought together in an abbey. Perhaps he too believes in Jung's meaningful coincidence: If you meet like this, it's because you're being given a chance. And possibly she's getting this chance right now. Perhaps she should get up, take a seat at his table, tell him about what she's caught up in. If he's sitting on his own and believes in meaningful coincidences it is quite possible that he would listen to her and not take what she is saying for madness. If he believes that an outside force can sometimes send things your way and therefore you have a responsibility to steward them, then he might minister to her, he might say that he has a room here and she can share it with him, he can sleep on the sofa and she in the bed or the other way around, and tomorrow they can walk through the hills and have lunch together, talk, and in peace and quiet examine the fact of their having been brought together. She thinks she can tell that the man across from her sees the divine in all this. Suddenly she thinks he looks ridiculous. Ridiculous hairstyle, a foolish glimmer in his eye. The kind of gaze that makes you want to bring things back down to earth. No, not bring, kick down to earth. By saying something dirty, shocking, and vulgar, and so puncturing the sublimity. Il pulito can do that. He is a master at puncturing all kinds of sublimity, all kinds of pathetic, stiff, and self-fulfilling sublimity, the likes of which abound in her home country, the likes of which make her want to vomit, the likes of which Il pulito can puncture with his blistering, matchless bravado. She feels a strong urge to cry. Unlike the hopeful man opposite her, she knows how things are, the lay of the land, and what will soon transpire. All she has to do is wait and catastrophe will come crashing in, and with it the magic this man is feeling will be mangled like a baby bird taken in hand and flung against a stone wall. Il pulito will come in, and the man's hopes will be dashed with breakneck speed. And this is precisely what happens. The front door opens and Il pulito enters the restaurant. No, he does not enter the restaurant, he rushes in, thunders, because he has kept her waiting much longer than a short while, a long while, perhaps a full hour, and he can tell that what should be a pleasant dinner is now in danger of being poisoned by her sour puss and then—on top of the defective shipment of brakes—he's going to have to deal with her as well. Still shouting into his phone, Il pulito's voice is a storm rumbling through the tranquil atmosphere, echoing throughout the old refectory. A radioactive aura of stress surrounds him. He hurries over to her, pressing the phone to his shoulder with one hand and holding the other out toward her, as if trying to fend off an attack.

He says, "I'm sorry, Minnie, please don't kill me, I'm almost done!"

He smiles apologetically at the people around as if to say, "That's an angry woman we have here, she's about to murder me." He finishes his call standing next to the table. People look at him with disgust. Il pulito is blocking her view of the man at the other table. Finally, Il pulito sits down, puts the phone in his pocket, and crosses his arms on the table. Then he smiles at her. His face is red, beads of sweat cling to his brow, and there are wet patches on his shirt, but he's smiling, even though the effort going into smiling like that must be substantial.

"Minnie," he says, "don't ruin the whole evening by being angry."

She smiles wanly. She's not about to get angry. He is torturing her, but she's not about to cry out, because if his torture makes her cry out, it will be taken as a kind of attack on him, and that won't do. *Stand by your man* and shut your mouth. Now she can see the man at the other table. He has stood up and is staring at her behind Il pulito's back. He looks like he can't believe his eyes and slowly shakes his head. Then he heads for the exit. Right before he leaves, he meets her gaze. She is trying to read his face, but can't tell if it's full of despair or fury.

THE FACT THAT she is doing her utmost not to provoke Il pulito shifts something in their dynamic. It's as if her obedience confirms that she has indeed committed a crime. For what else would give rise to such obedience, if not a sense of guilt? And if there is a sense of guilt, there is guilt, and if there is guilt, there is of course a crime. She sees the logic of the causal chain. She also understands that this conviction gives rise to a low-intensity rage in him, a seething rage below the surface, that threatens to catch fire and explode at any second. Every now and then, however, he also seems to be pulling himself together and making an effort not to give in to his anger. One evening, for example, in a rage, he drives his hand straight into the wall. Instead of hitting her, he hits the cement in his apartment. However, the cement is significantly harder than she is, and he grimaces in pain. The conclusion he draws from this is that she is the cause of his days-long pain. She provoked his anger, he *protected* her by punching the wall in her stead, and suffered personal injury. His anger is exacerbated. Layer is added upon layer. With each of her minor missteps, the rage intensifies. She can hear the rumbling of the abyss ever more clearly.

One night he says, "Then there's the issue of class, Minnie."

"What do you mean?"

"You and me, we don't come from the same place."

"True."

"You've always thought you were a tiny bit better than me."

"No. That's not true."

"Yes, it is. You've gone to university, you come from a family where people have gone to university."

"We weren't richer than anyone else."

"Your family had other things. You had *opportunities*."

She leans back in the armchair, sets the book she's reading on the coffee table. And then she starts laughing. Like when she was trapped in a cage in New Orleans, she laughs. Her laughter is loud, mocking, and long.

"What is it?" he says in a huff.

"Just drop it," she says, "just drop the whole class bit."

"Why?"

"Because I say so."

"Because you say so?"

"Yes."

"What do you know about these things?"

"Enough."

"Explain yourself, Minnie."

"It's like this. First, I came from a nice family. But then we moved to the countryside, to a village full of *white trash*, and that's where I grew up, those were the people who shaped me. But when I got there, they thought, like you, that I was putting on airs. I adapted, because that's what children do, they adapt because they want to be like everybody else. I became like them. Then I grew up, eventually ended up in the capital, and there they thought I was too unrefined, too ugly, that I came from some hole out in the country where only pervs and pedophiles live. They looked down on me and shut me out as best they could. So as far as class is concerned, Mickey, let's just drop it, because it's beyond our sphere of influence. We're either too refined or too rough and somewhere out there, a very small group of people are sitting around deciding how these things fit together. The best you and I can do is stick together, have as nice a time as we can, fight our own battles, and try to mind our own business."

He nods. He even smiles a little. "True, Minnie, true."

The danger is momentarily averted. But once again she realizes that she needs assistance. If she's going to handle Il pulito, if she's going to neutralize his anger, and seriously build something with him after what happened in New Orleans, she needs a better understanding of what makes him tick and how she can get him to stop hating her. She considers going back to la dottoressa. Then she thinks that she should be able to read her way to a solution, and so she downloads a number of self-help books from Amazon. *Get Over Betrayal in 14 Days* by Bhumi Desai, *Healing from Hidden Abuse* by Shannon Thomas, *The Victim Addiction* by Victoria Lee Carlyle, and a book on how Zen Buddhist prayer can repair trauma. She digs in, but soon tires. Everything in the books sounds good, but none of it sticks. The examples given are all different from her own, the circumstances described do not apply to her case. They can't help her. The books are like life buoys bobbing near the shore, but she is too far out at sea to reach them. She stops reading and again considers a second visit to la dottoressa.

ON ONE OF these nights she dreams that she is sleeping beside her demon. She can't see the demon's face, but she can feel its presence, a presence that emits such a chill she fumbles for the covers. I'm so cold, she whispers, I'm freezing. Where's the blanket? Her words come out garbled, as if she were still in a dream. Then she hears the demon's voice in the bedroom. It says, "Don't you know there's only one way to survive in extreme cold?"

"And what's that?" she asks.

"To assume an even lower temperature yourself."

She wakes up. An icy draft blows through the open window.

SO ONE DAY when Il pulito comes home from work, he says, "Minnie, sit down. I've got it all figured out now."

"Oh?"

He takes off his shoes, puts his keys in the bookcase, and goes into the bathroom to wash his hands. When he comes out, he takes the bunch of keys and locks the front door.

"Why are you locking it?" she says.

"Just listen," he says, and puts the keys in his pocket. "Just listen."

This must be some kind of game, she thinks. Something he heard about during the day at work, a game some colleague played with his partner and that he now wants to try out with her. He pulls out a chair at the kitchen table and takes a seat in front of her.

"I want you to listen carefully to what I have to say and to think carefully before you react. I promise that what is about to happen won't hurt you one bit."

"Okay," she says. "I'm listening. Go on."

"I've been thinking for a while now, Minnie, ever since we

came back from the States, and I've figured it out. I don't want to go into detail, but it involves an operation."

"An operation? What kind of operation?"

"An operation that will make it impossible for you to be so damn passionate."

She doesn't understand. What does he mean? An operation that makes a person less passionate?

"A lobotomy?"

Il pulito laughs. "No, not quite that dramatic. Lower down."

"Lower down?"

"Below the navel but above the thighs."

She stares at him and feels her pulse quicken. "You mean—"

He holds up a hand. "Don't say it. It sounds so barbaric."

He must be joking. This is a joke. An unpleasant joke. She has to keep a cool head. She can try to evade the subject if she starts at a different place. Her throat has tightened but she clears it and says as firmly as she can, "What do you mean when you say I'm 'so passionate'?"

"Well, so, I've really tried to believe that you're not, but even at the abbey, Minnie, even when I was going around trying to avert disaster with that French manufacturer, you sat there in that cozy room letting another man treat you to glass after glass of wine."

"What do you mean?"

"I could see it from outside, through the window. You were being given one glass of wine after the next, and a man at another table was looking at you the whole time. Do you think I'm fucking stupid? You might think you can dupe Mickey, but you can't. You're not smarter than I am. I saw everything, and at first I thought maybe you ordered those glasses yourself, as consolation for being left to sit on your own, but when I went to pay I saw that they weren't on the bill. It's not hard to put two and two together, Minnie. It's not hard to put two and two together."

She shakes her head. No, no. Is he out of his mind? She got the wine from Giovanni, the owner. It was *on the house.* Il pulito shakes his head with a wry smile.

"Oh Minnie," he says, "Minnie . . . haven't you learned anything? You lusty piece of ass. Sitting there, checking out another man while Mickey is trying to put out a fire . . . haven't you learned *anything*?"

She feels the panic come creeping. The demon got the better of her. She thought she was safe in that sacred place, but the demon grabbed her by foot and now she's stumbling, she's crashing face-first into the cobbles. She has to breathe, has to keep calm. Talk to Il pulito, at least he's still calm, he's sitting there looking at her with compassion, which is good, he's not angry, he's not going to do anything violent, not yet, not right now. She clears her throat again and again, trying to dislodge some phlegm. She says, first of all, he can call the abbey and ask. Ask Giovanni about the wine, he'll clear this up. Second, how passionate is she really? Thirdly, the solution he has proposed is far too brutal, there's no rhyme or reason to it. Il pulito nods with a smile that she can only describe as shimmering. Sure, he says, he knows, but they won't do it *that* way. After all, the most barbaric part is the pain, right? The pain won't be an issue. He has already spoken to a doctor. A doctor? Doctors don't do that kind of thing, do they? This doctor does, accommodating requests that are on the shadow side of the law is right in his wheelhouse. She gets up and rushes to the door, but of course, it's locked. She looks to the window, but Il pulito gets up, walks over, and shuts it.

"You will be put under," he reiterates, "don't you worry. Everything will be perfectly hygienic, no worse than a boob job, and those get done all the time. They put you under. When you wake up, you'll be somebody else, when you wake up, it will finally be just the two of us."

"I don't understand," she says. "You came all the way to New Orleans to save me, and now you want to do *this*?"

"It's because I love you, Minnie. Despite everything you've done to me and still do to me when the opportunity arises, I love you."

"This isn't healthy."

"Healthy?" he says with a laugh. "What a funny word, considering all you've done."

She has to get out. No, that's not possible. She'll scream. If she screams, he'll presumably beat her until she passes out. So she can't scream. She needs a different plan, a better plan, a plan with neither screaming nor resistance. A plan where you use your opponent's strength against them. To do that, she must lie, and to lie well, one must believe the lie. In order to communicate with Il pulito now, she must think like him. To communicate, she must do what la dottoressa failed to do: Speak the patient's language. Jung and the cancerous tumor. A mad person comes up with a solution to a problem. Even if it is a brutal solution, it is a solution that the mad person has thought up because he is convinced it will work. Part of the madness is that the mad person believes that other people might also think it will work, and it is in this realm of madness that she must encounter him.

"It's just that," she says as calm as can be, "it feels so . . . grotesque."

"Yes, true. But then again, it's been grotesque all along, in various ways, hasn't it? I mean, just think of how you went on and on about demons."

Keep cool. Pretend he's right, pretend the demons don't exist. She's trying to visualize the various planes on which the conversation is taking place. It's like splitting the brain into different parts, and this is exactly what she must do: Split into multiple planes. One plane that belongs to them, Mickey and Minnie, and then one to the demons, and one to the demons via the two of them. This demands of her synchronous comprehension—how are they communicating, and how are the demons communicating through them? It's like listening to parallel conversations and making strategic decisions while those multiple conversations are ongoing. The demon in him is trying to outsmart the demon in her, the demons want to kill each other and they will not rest until one of them is dead. To succeed, she must reason with herself as if Il pulito's proposal were reasonable. She remembers trying to get out of the cage at Hector's and thinking that it didn't matter if that particular part of her got destroyed. This thought originated with her, right? Yes, but she was also trapped, drugged, confused, which has an effect on your thinking. Isn't making a sacrifice part of getting free? Like a shackled person in a burning building cutting off their hand to get free? But isn't she sacrificing one thing in order to get another now, isn't that exactly the way Il pulito is seeing it? Yes, right, and that's how she must see it, too, this is the logic she must adopt. She will make him think that she's seeing things the way he's seeing them, and then outsmart him.

"Okay," she says, "I'll come with you. We'll do as you say. I have to trust you. I trusted you when you told me to be weak and put myself in your hands, and that didn't work out particularly well, but for our sake and for everything that's at stake now, I'll do it again. It's mad, but I'm going to do it anyway. And if it's done clinically and painlessly at a medical center like you say it will be, then there's no risk. I'll go with you, I trust that it's a good decision. The doctor will remove a part of me, but he'll do so with skill, and I won't be missing anything. Now that I think about it, I'm actually tired of my own desire, because in the end, it's what got us into this mess. If I have no desire, maybe I won't feel jealousy either. On closer consideration, then, I welcome your decision."

At first Il pulito looks like he's assessing her. He looks her in the eye and it is as if he is trying to plumb her depths, to see into her innermost thoughts and intentions. Is she manipulating him? Suddenly she feels the coldness of the being standing before her, and it makes her want to scream. Her throat tightens and icy shivers run along her spine, but her gaze does not waver. Finally, Il pulito's face cracks into a smile, and he nods.

"Good, Minnie. We'll take care of this, we'll make sure everything's in order. All right, let's go."

"Now?"

She feels a cold sweat in her armpits.

"Some things shouldn't be thought about for too long. When a good idea pops up, run with it, otherwise things might deadlock."

"True. But maybe we should sleep on it, anyway?"

He smiles. "I can tell you're trying to bargain for time, Minnie. But it's already been decided, booked. We're going. They're waiting for us."

"I see. Let me just get a few things. How long will we be gone?"

"A couple of days at most."

She packs a small bag of clothes from the closet, takes her toothbrush from the bathroom. He keeps a tight grip on her arm as they walk down the stairs, locks the car once they're in their seats. She looks straight ahead, at the road. She notices that he's keeping an eye on her, as if he's still trying to figure out if she's manipulating him or if she's actually being sincere. But because she's sitting in the passenger seat so still, so straight and amenable, it's as if she is in fact in agreement that this is the best course of action for her, for the both of them. She knows that this is coming as a surprise to him, because she is now the slave, the slave who has observed the master and drawn her lessons, and without noticing it himself the master has slipped down to a lower position whereas the slave has glided up, because the master does not understand, the master has not spent much time in the edgelands—there he would have been forced to sharpen his awareness—but the slave has, she has. The only way to survive extreme cold is to assume an even lower temperature yourself. Isn't that what the demon inside her said? And the soul, what does it say? She tries to feel around inside her for what could be the soul. The quiet self-evidence about which Jung wrote. If the soul exists, and she has always believed that it does, it must come to her aid now. In order to do what she must now do, she has to know that the soul exists and that this is the right thing to do. She closes her eyes, tries to turn her gaze inward. The demon is there, but so is her soul. Hot, alive. Coherent, tacit, and also inciting action.

Il pulito turns the music on. It's a fine afternoon, they zip almost soundlessly past the fields outside Florence. They're not far from Montecatini when she turns to him and hisses that one of his whores lives here, in Montecatini, doesn't she? If she remembers correctly, it was in this damned village, this godforsaken speck on the map, that he once turned up, cock in hand, to stick it to a married woman with three children, does he know what that would have meant in Mussolini's time? Well, it would have been adultery pure and simple and he would have been punished like the horndog he is. She's screaming as she grabs hold of the handbrake and yanks it. The car stops with a jolt. Il pulito looks at her in fury, eyes bulging out of their sockets. And did he really think he would get to cut off her most sacred part, did he really think he would get to *mutilate* her, how will she be able to screw around when it's over between them, how will she be able to go around and *prendere cazzi in giro*, fucking anything that comes her way, what joy would there be in it for her then? He's a proper idiot, you can see it in his cloudy eyes and you can smell it on his scalp when he's sleeping, because that's when it vaporizes, the stupidity, that's when it diffuses into the room and even if every single one of his whores set to work draining him of bodily fluids twenty-four hours a day every day for the rest of his life, even then the poison that his scalp secretes couldn't be broken down.

She catches her breath. Il pulito's gaze is ice-cold and his face has turned white, as if emptied of blood. He puts his hand on her thigh and says softly and with menace, his voice like a razor blade wrapped in warm cotton, "You have a death wish, don't you, Minnie? You've come all the way from New Orleans, you've let Mickey bring you home, to die?"

"You're pathetic," is her reply. "I feel *sorry* for you!"

She looks away, crosses her arms over her chest, and stares straight ahead, at the road. Il pulito starts the engine, shifts into gear, accelerates. She looks at the speedometer, watches it climb to 70, then 80, and soon they're up to 110. They leave the motorway, navigate a roundabout, and are soon in Montecatini. But she can also feel the uncertainty in Il pulito's handling, because deep down he doesn't want to die, he wasn't prepared for this, this wasn't his intent when he opened the door to this situation, and even if he does want to kill her now, he doesn't want to die himself. From where she's sitting she knows that he's thinking about everything he'll lose if he dies, and who would miss him, and what he'd miss out on. She knows, because the slave knows, and the slave says, "You're driving like a fucking bitch, who'd have thought: A guy like you driving like an old bitch. Where's your manhood? Have they castrated you too?"

She has crossed the line. Il pulito floors it and they're off like a shot through the next intersection. A truck comes hurtling toward them and the driver must have sounded the horn because she hears the signal, so drawn out, so harsh, closer and closer until her eardrum bursts with a howl. And it is then, in that split second and yet in slow motion, when the metal body of the car drives into their bodies like the blades of many swords, it is when the steel and iron melts in flames around them, that she thinks she hears their laughter. Two loud, lusty laughs rising to the heavens in a euphoria that can only be demonic. So they weren't trying to kill each other, she realizes, they wanted to kill us. And this is the devil's grip, she also realizes, that's what is releasing now, now that it's too late the grip is releasing, it's releasing right now, because she senses the words coming back to her, suddenly she can once again perform her recitations, *è la presa del diavolo, es el agarre del diablo*, the words have come back to her because the grip has been released. Before the tremendous pain drives its awls into their flesh, she has time to feel this great relief and she looks Il pulito in the eye and hopes he feels it too, wants him to share in this understanding, to understand that the end has come, they are free now, and she knows that he would only need another split second, one split second more for the realization to take hold. But this does not come to pass, for in the eyes of Il pulito she only sees horror and pain and knows that she cannot warm him, she cannot do anything for him even though inside her she feels all the forgiveness that only a human heart, once more unsullied, can hold.